# Enrollment Form

☐ **Yes!** I WANT TO BE A *Privileged Woman*.

Enclosed is one *PAGES & PRIVILEGES*™ Proof of Purchase from any Harlequin or Silhouette book currently for sale in stores (Proofs of Purchase are found on the back pages of books) and the store cash register receipt. Please enroll me in *PAGES & PRIVILEGES*™. Send my Welcome Kit and FREE Gifts -- and activate my FREE benefits -- immediately.

*More great gifts and benefits to come.*

NAME (please print)

ADDRESS                                                          APT. NO

CITY                          STATE                   ZIP/POSTAL CODE

PROOF OF PURCHASE
SAMPLE ONLY
Pages & Privileges

**NO CLUB!**
**NO COMMITMENT!**
*Just one purchase brings you great Free Gifts and Benefits!*

Please allow 6-8 weeks for delivery. Quantities are limited. We reserve the right to substitute items. Enroll before October 31, 1995 and receive one full year of benefits.

Name of store where this book was purchased_____

Date of purchase_____

Type of store:
☐ Bookstore    ☐ Supermarket    ☐ Drugstore
☐ Dept. or discount store (e.g. K-Mart or Walmart)
☐ Other (specify)_____

Which Harlequin or Silhouette series do you usually read?

_____

**Complete and mail with one Proof of Purchase and store receipt to:**
**U.S.:** *PAGES & PRIVILEGES*™, P.O. Box 1960, Danbury, CT 06813-1960
**Canada:** *PAGES & PRIVILEGES*™, 49-6A The Donway West, P.O. 813, North York, ON M3C 2E8

SR-PP6B

### "You really believe a woman can use her wiles to make a man weak with desire?"

Miranda asked.

Stuart nodded, his eyes narrowed.

"Have you ever wanted anyone that much?"

"No. And I never will. No lying, scheming woman is going to make a fool out of me."

"Oh, no?" Miranda purred, stepping close and sliding her arms around his neck. "Well, you don't have to worry about me."

"Don't I?" When she tried to move toward him, he held her in place. He didn't want her to get closer.

"No, you don't."

"You don't want anything from me?"

She reached up to stroke his jaw. "I didn't say *that*."

Dear Reader,

Favorite author Kasey Michaels starts off the month with another irresistible FABULOUS FATHER in *The Dad Next Door*. Quinn Patrick was enjoying a carefree bachelor life-style until Maddie Pemberton and her son, Dillon, moved next door. And suddenly Quinn was faced with the prospect of a ready-made family!

A BUNDLE OF JOY helps two people find love in *Temporarily Hers* by Susan Meier. Katherine Whitman would do anything to win custody of her nephew, Jason, even marry playboy Alex Cane—temporarily. But soon Katherine found herself wishing their marriage was more than a temporary arrangement....

Favorite author Anne Peters gives us the second installment in her miniseries FIRST COMES MARRIAGE. Joy Cooper needed a *Stand-in Husband* to save her reputation. Who better for the job than Paul Mallik, the stranger she had rescued from the sea? Of course, love was never supposed to enter the picture!

The spirit of the West lives on in Pat Montana's *Storybook Cowboy*. Jo McPherson didn't want to trust Trey Covington, the upstart cowboy who stirred her heart. If she wasn't careful, she might find herself in love with the handsome scoundrel!

This month, we're delighted to present our PREMIERE AUTHOR, Linda Lewis, debuting with a fun-filled, fast-paced love story, *Honeymoon Suite*. And rounding out the month, look for Dani Criss's exciting romance, *Family Ties*.

Happy Reading!

Anne Canadeo, Senior Editor

Please address questions and book requests to:
Silhouette Reader Service
U.S.: 3010 Walden Ave., P.O. Box 1325, Buffalo, NY 14269
Canadian: P.O. Box 609, Fort Erie, Ont. L2A 5X3

# HONEYMOON SUITE

## Linda Lewis

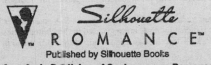

Silhouette
R O M A N C E™
Published by Silhouette Books
America's Publisher of Contemporary Romance

To Gloria Alvarez and Jo Ann Vest for the Gulf Coast Writers' Retreats in Perdido Key, and to Metsy Hingle, Janet Milkovich and Erica Spindler for the Plantation Coffee House critiques.

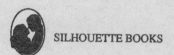 SILHOUETTE BOOKS

ISBN 0-373-19113-8

HONEYMOON SUITE

Copyright © 1995 by Linda Kay West

**Printed in U.S.A.**

## LINDA LEWIS

was born and raised in Texas. She lived in New York, Philadelphia and Chicago before settling down in New Orleans. Linda is an attorney and resides with her family and an embarrassing number of dogs and cats.

Dear Reader,

Being Silhouette Romance's Premiere author for 1995 is better than a dream come true! After taking a course called "How to Write A Romance Novel" taught by Emilie Richards and Karen Young, both of whom were writing for Silhouette Romance at the time (1987), my goal was to follow in their footsteps.

That dream became reality when editor Melissa Jeglinski called me and said she wanted to buy *Honeymoon Suite*. The Premiere author designation is *lagniappe*—something extra—as we say in New Orleans, and made a very happy event even more special.

I had finished three manuscripts before this first sale. The heroine of the first book I completed practiced tax law, since that's what I do in my day job. When that book didn't sell, I decided "writing what you know" was a rule made to be broken. The setting, characters and story for *Honeymoon Suite* are all products of my imagination. "Writing what you don't know" turned out to be a lot more fun. How else could I have hobnobbed with movie stars and Broadway actresses, traveled to a Caribbean island in search of stolen jewels and lost my heart to the thief?

I hope you enjoy the trip to San Sebastian as much as I did. I'd love to receive your comments. Please write me at P.O. Box 6098, New Orleans, Louisiana 70174.

*Linda Lewis*

# Prologue

Maude Merrick swept into the room in a manner befitting the acknowledged queen of the American stage. She walked into the arms of Tynan Rafferty St. James, the silver-haired star of the season's hit television series. When he'd enclosed her in his embrace, she said, in the voice that made even hardened critics weep, "Darling Tynan, I'm so glad you're finally here in New York. How was your flight?"

"Don't chitchat, Maude. I'm not here to discuss my flight or the weather. What have you done with Miranda?"

"Miranda?"

"Our daughter. Where is she?"

Maude took Tynan's left hand and pushed up his shirt sleeve. She looked at his thin gold wristwatch and said, "She should be arriving on San Sebastian in a few more hours." Releasing his hand, she lowered herself gracefully onto the rose brocade sofa.

"San Sebastian?" Tynan asked, joining Maude on the couch. "Isn't that the place your last husband kicked the bucket?"

"Don't be crude, darling. Yes, San Sebastian is where I lost dear Robert." Maude sniffed as she leaned over and took the monogrammed handkerchief from Tynan's breast pocket. She dabbed at the corners of her blue-green eyes and gave a dramatic sigh.

"You're overacting, Maude. You only do that when you're up to no good. *Why* is Miranda on her way to San Sebastian?"

"She's running a little errand for me, that's all," Maude said with an airy wave of her hand.

"What errand?"

"She's going to get my jewelry—I left it behind when I returned to New York after Robert's death."

"You left your jewelry behind? All those pretty rocks you've accumulated over the years? How could you have forgotten them?"

"We left so suddenly when Robert had his heart attack—I went on the helicopter with him, of course."

"Of course. But you've been a widow for more than a year. Why haven't you gone back for the trinkets?"

Maude raised a perfectly formed eyebrow. "I've been otherwise occupied."

"With the play. I understand. You couldn't leave town while giving eight performances a week in the hit of the season." Tynan dropped another kiss on the corner of her prettily pouting mouth. "Couldn't you have asked someone to send your jewelry to you? Don't you have a stepson living there?"

Maude sighed. "Yes. Stuart Winslow. He's a handsome devil, like his father. But Stuart never liked me. He had the ridiculous opinion that actresses are nothing more than paid liars."

"All actresses, or just you?"

Maude bristled. "I beg your pardon."

Tynan patted her shoulder. "Now, Maude, you know you sometimes embellish the truth."

"Only when it's dull. Stuart never appreciated my attempts to make life more interesting. All he ever wanted was a dry recital of the facts."

"A stickler for the truth?" Tynan grinned. "No wonder you didn't get along."

"We didn't have to get along—he wasn't around that much. But when Robert died, Stuart blamed me. Just because his father and I were in bed together before...oh, dear. That wasn't very tactful of me, was it?"

"I don't mind if you talk about your ex-husbands—especially the dead ones—now that you're wearing my engagement ring. Why won't Stuart send you the jewels?"

"Oh, he doesn't know about them. They're in a safe I had installed at Sugar House while Robert was away. No one knows about the jewels or the safe."

"You talked our daughter into cracking a safe?" Tynan let loose a hearty guffaw. "I don't believe it. Miranda won't cross the street when the sign says don't walk. She'd never commit a felony."

"She's not going to break the law or the safe. I gave her the combination. All she has to do is get into the master bedroom at Sugar House."

"Let me get this straight. Miranda has to get the jewels from a safe in your bedroom?"

Maude nodded. "Except it's Stuart's bedroom now."

"So you, my darling, taught Miranda how to get into a man's bedroom?"

"Exactly."

"Maude?" A gleam lit Tynan's blue eyes. "Did you teach her how to get out?"

# Chapter One

"It looks like my career as a jewel thief is about to come to an end."

Stuart Winslow crumpled the copy of the passenger list he'd been reading and tossed it onto his desk. At this very moment, Miranda St. James was on board the yacht sailing to San Sebastian from Montego Bay.

"You are not a thief!" Pauline Winslow insisted. "You only borrowed—"

"I took something that didn't belong to me, Aunt Polly." Stuart leaned back in his chair and looked at the trim, middle-aged woman seated across from him. "The fact that I don't intend to keep it doesn't change that."

He never should have told Polly about the jewels, Stuart decided. No matter how much he'd needed someone's approval for what he'd done, he shouldn't have burdened his proper aunt with the knowledge of his crime. After all, Polly was the one who'd taught him right from wrong. His parents hadn't had time to give him morality lessons.

"What you did hasn't harmed anyone, Stuart. And it helped a great number of people—all the Island International employees, including me. If it weren't for this job, I—I might be a bag lady."

Stuart frowned, surprised at the uncharacteristic heat in Polly's voice. What had happened to the woman who was normally as cool and orderly as her silver-gray chignon?

"Bag lady? I don't think so, Polly." She would survive without Island International. He was the one driven by the need to keep intact the empire his father had built. If he failed, Robert Winslow's life would have had no meaning. And neither would his own.

"There's no mistake, is there?" Polly asked anxiously. "Miranda St. James is Maude's daughter, isn't she?"

Stuart gave her a rueful grin. "She's Maude's daughter, all right." He shoved away from his desk. "Damn! Less than two months from making crime pay and she has to turn up."

"What are you going to do?"

"I don't know yet."

"If only I'd seen her reservation request! We could have said the resort was booked."

"At least we know she's on the way—thanks to you. I'd almost forgotten Maude had a daughter."

"She wasn't at the wedding, was she?" asked Polly.

"No. And she never visited Maude. Dad said Miranda didn't approve of the marriage."

"You have that in common, then." Polly straightened an already perfectly aligned stack of papers on the corner of his desk, then looked up. "Which one of Maude's husbands is her father? I don't recall a St. James."

"The first one—Tynan Rafferty. He dropped the St. James surname years ago."

"Really? Those show business people change their names as freely as they change their mates, don't they?"

Aunt Polly looked more fascinated than disapproving, he thought. Maybe because she'd never married. "Even for an actress, Maude overdid the mate changing," he said.

"Let's see if I can remember the others. First Rafferty, then that Broadway producer, followed by the Irish playwright and finally Robert." Polly gave him a triumphant grin.

"I doubt Dad will have been Maude's final husband," Stuart said wryly. "How did you spot her daughter's name?"

"I was looking at the passenger list to see if that nanny Bill and Cathy hired made the boat. She didn't. We'll have to keep using staff to watch after Tommy, at least until the yacht makes a return trip next week."

"I don't see why the woman wouldn't let me send the helicopter for her. What kind of nanny doesn't like to fly?"

"The only unemployed nanny on Jamaica, apparently. Anyway, I was looking for her name—Beatrice Sullivan—when I saw Miranda St. James. The name was familiar to me because Robert mentioned her once or twice."

"Yeah. Dad told me a few things about her, too."

Polly took off her wire-rimmed glasses and polished them with a lace-edged handkerchief. "Maybe we're reading too much into her visit. She could be just another hardworking young woman taking a vacation from her job.''

''Vacation? Polly, her job *is* a vacation.''

''She's not in the hotel business then.''

''You got that right,'' Stuart said. ''She has a job I'd kill for—cataloging Waldo Wisdom's film collection.''

''Waldo Wisdom. Wasn't he the last of the great movie moguls?''

''Yep. His film collection includes every great and not-so-great movie from the twenties through the sixties.''

''No wonder you covet her job. Honestly, Stuart! You're the only man I know who'd rather spend Saturday night with a celluloid image instead of a live woman.''

Stuart leaned forward and grinned. ''Ah, but what images. I've never met a real woman who could compete with Rita Hayworth, Ava Gardner—''

''Maude Merrick?''

Stuart's grin changed to a grimace. ''Maude is too real. So is her daughter. Did you check her reservation? How long is she going to be with us?''

''Two weeks.'' Polly handed him a copy of the reservation record.

He scanned it quickly. ''Waldo Wisdom's estate must pay well. She requested a four-hundred-dollar-a-night suite.''

''Maybe she's counting on a family discount.''

''She didn't ask for one, did she?''

''No. There's no mention of the relationship in her letter requesting reservations.''

''She didn't use her full name, either.'' At his aunt's questioning glance, he added, ''It's Miranda *Merrick* St. James.''

''You're sure Maude's behind this?''

"I'd bet my movie collection on it. For one thing, if Miranda can't afford the suite, Maude can." Stuart had to smile. "If she remembers to pay for it."

He had reason to know that, even without her fabled jewelry collection, Maude was a wealthy woman. Her several husbands—his father among them—had seen to that. The bill from San Sebastian would not be a financial burden for Robert Winslow's widow.

Stuart's smile widened. His former stepmother's problem with paying bills wasn't lack of funds but lack of interest. Maude had always relied on others to take care of mundane chores like paying tradespeople. If she hadn't been so charmingly dependent in matters of finance, he'd never have known about the safe.

Yes, he was fortunate that the locksmith had presented a bill to him shortly after his father's untimely death. He hadn't paid the invoice until the locksmith had explained that Maude had ordered a safe installed under the fireplace hearth in the master bedroom at Sugar House. The man had been so glad to get his money that he'd put the combination to the safe on the receipt for payment.

Stuart sat back in his chair and stared out the window, recalling how he'd filed the receipt away and gone on to deal with all the problems he'd unexpectedly inherited. He'd been too distracted by grief and the prospect of managing Island International to be even mildly curious about why Maude had needed a secret safe.

He should have guessed. He'd heard of her cache of jewels—the whole world knew about the Merrick collection. It rivaled those of Elizabeth Taylor and the Duchess of Windsor.

Still, he never would have connected Maude's jewels with the safe in his bedroom. Treasures like that belonged in a bank vault, not in a private home—no matter how good a security system it boasted. But that's exactly where he'd found the jewelry when he'd finally gotten around to opening the safe.

He'd taken the jewels. Stolen them, to be blunt. He could at least be honest with himself about his crime. And it was a crime, even on San Sebastian where he was the law.

He could have used his ownership of the island to keep Maude away, but it hadn't been necessary up to now. She hadn't tried to return to San Sebastian since the funeral. Maude Merrick had come out of retirement—and mourning—a few short weeks after his father's death. She'd spent the past year reestablishing her career on Broadway.

Damn! Stuart cursed silently. He'd thought he was safe, at least until *Future Perfect*, Maude's latest play, closed. He hadn't anticipated Maude sending her daughter after the jewels.

"She's coming for Maude's jewels, isn't she?" Polly echoed his thoughts.

"Of course."

"What are we going to do?"

"Keep her away from me. She can't get to the safe unless she gets to me first."

Miranda leaned against the boat rail and watched as the gray-green haze on the horizon gradually coalesced into an island. Not just any island—San Sebastian, the setting for her very first starring role. She wasn't sure whether the tremors shimmying along her nerve endings were caused by excitement or stage fright or both.

Why hadn't Maude told her how to deal with this? She'd covered everything else. Miranda smiled as she re-

called her last conversation with her mother. They'd been
in the limousine on the way to Kennedy Airport and
Maude had been grilling her like a pilot going through a
preflight checklist.

"Where is Stuart's bedroom?"

"Second floor, first door on the left."

"The safe?"

"Beneath the fireplace hearth, under the second stone
from the wall."

"Combination?"

"One, five, forty-nine. I won't forget, Mother."

"I should hope not. It is my birthday, after all."

"I'm clear on everything, Mother," Miranda said,
without much hope of stemming Maude's monologue.
She giggled. Maybe she could sell it. *Maude Merrick's
Checklist for Seduction.*

Maude raised an eyebrow. "Don't giggle, Miranda.
Girlish giggling will not appeal to Stuart. He's a very serious man."

Miranda sucked in her cheeks. "Sorry, Mother," she
gurgled.

"Looking like a goldfish out of water won't attract
him, either. What is so funny?"

Miranda gave up and howled with glee. After a few
moments, Maude laughed along with her.

"I'm sorry," Miranda repeated as soon as she could
talk again. "Go on."

"Pay attention, Miranda. Stuart won't be easy. He's
like his father. A workaholic. He sets goals, makes plans.
Actually, he's worse than his father. Robert at least had
time for me."

"You're sure this is the best way to do this?"

"Do what, dear?" Maude took a gold compact out of
her purse. "This tiny little favor?"

"Yes, Mother. I don't mind getting your jewels for you—"

"And a paid vacation at the newest Island International resort." Maude opened the compact and studied her reflection.

"Right. I'm sure I'll have a wonderful time. But—"

"We're almost at the airport."

"Is it really necessary for me to lie about who I am?"

"I'd hardly call it a lie. You are using your real name."

"But no one ever remembers my real name. You know that." For years Miranda had answered to Miranda Merrick or Miranda Rafferty, depending on which parent she was living with at the time. She'd spent a good number of those years wishing she was part of a family where everyone had the same last name.

"I'm counting on it. I'm sure Stuart won't know who you are."

"Would it matter so much if he did? Why can't I just tell him about the safe and ask permission to get the jewels out of it?"

"Because." Maude turned her turquoise eyes on Miranda. "Besides, I'd have thought you'd prefer keeping your identity a secret. You never want people to know I'm your mother. Sometimes I think you're ashamed of me."

"Mother! You know that's not true. I just get tired of people fawning over me to get to you or Daddy. Once they know who my parents are, they want me to ask you for an audition, tickets to *Future Perfect,* something. I hate that."

"You're too sensitive, Miranda. I've told you time and again that I don't mind doing things for your friends."

"But I never know if they really are my friends, or if they're just using me to get to you."

"I know, dear. Tynan told me about that lawyer you were dating last year—what was his name? The one who wanted to renegotiate your father's contract with the network."

Miranda turned and looked out the window. "Daniel Eberhart." Daniel had worked for the law firm that handled Waldo Wisdom's estate. That assignment had whetted his appetite for a show business clientele—starting with Tynan and Maude. Daniel had revealed his real interest before Miranda's heart had been seriously threatened, but the experience had left her with doubts about her judgment concerning the opposite sex.

"Don't worry, Miranda. Some day you'll fall in love with a man who'll love you back, someone who won't care who your parents are."

Miranda turned and gave her mother an indulgent smile. "I'm not interested in falling in love."

"Nonsense. You are my daughter. Your experience with Daniel left you a little insecure, that's all. Your trip to San Sebastian will bolster your confidence. Once you have Stuart wrapped around your little finger, you'll know it's possible for a man to be attracted to you for yourself alone." Maude paused. "As long as you don't tell him who you are, of course."

"Shrewd, mother—giving me my own reason to do this caper undercover."

A satisfied smile curved Maude's lips. "I thought so. Besides, you'd be giving yourself a handicap if you told Stuart who you are. He doesn't like Merrick women."

"Merrick women? He only knows one of us. And he doesn't know you that well, does he? I thought he only came to San Sebastian once or twice while you were there."

"Trust me. I know Stuart well enough to understand he never approved of me. He thought I married his father for his money."

"Well, didn't you?"

"I've been pursued by many rich men, Miranda. I haven't married all of them."

"Yet," Miranda muttered.

"I heard that."

"Sorry, Mother." Miranda leaned back into the plush upholstery and grinned at Maude. "Even if Stuart didn't approve of you, why would he keep your jewelry? You said he was an honest man."

"Disgustingly so. Robert despaired of him at times. Dealing with the public requires tact. Tact and the truth aren't always compatible."

"Well, the truth is those jewels are yours, even if Robert did leave Sugar House and its contents to his son. He couldn't have meant your jewels. He didn't know you'd stashed them there." Miranda gave her mother a speculative look. "Why didn't you tell Robert about the safe? Didn't you trust him?"

"Of course I trusted Robert—as much as I've ever trusted any man."

Not much, then, thought Miranda, still leaning back into the plush upholstery. She and her mother had watched three men walk out the door. Even an eternal optimist like Maude must have learned not to put too much faith in a man by the time she'd married Robert Winslow. Miranda really couldn't blame Maude for not wanting to trust his son.

"I still wish you'd never met Robert Winslow. If you hadn't married him two years ago, you and Daddy—"

"—would have remarried that much sooner. I know you think that, darling, but it's not true."

"Isn't it?"

"No. Your father and I weren't in love with each other two years ago. If you remember, your father was pursuing that redheaded soap star then."

"Not very hard—he didn't catch her."

"And two years ago, I was in love with Robert," Maude said firmly.

"Yes, Mother." Miranda sighed. She should know better than to argue with Maude about love and marriage. Despite three divorces—and recent widowhood—Maude still believed in both.

"My marriage to Robert wasn't what kept Tynan and I apart. We simply weren't ready for each other two years ago. His television series had just started, if you recall. My marriage to Robert did keep you and me apart, though." Maude patted her on the knee. "I missed you, sweety."

Guilt made Miranda squirm. "I missed you, too. I acted like such a brat back then—not going to your wedding, refusing to see you for a whole year."

"Never mind. You were there when I really needed you, after Robert died. I don't know what I would have— oh, we're here."

The limousine glided to a smooth stop in front of the terminal. The driver opened the door for Miranda, then went to get her luggage from the trunk. Before she left the limo, Miranda gave Maude a fierce hug. "Don't worry, Mother. I'll get your jewels back."

"I know you will, darling. And you'll do it without telling Stuart who you are. Promise me?"

"I won't tell. I promise."

A flurry of activity from the yacht crew brought Miranda out of her reverie. She'd better stop rehashing Maude's instructions and get on with it. The show was about to begin, and she still hadn't decided who she should be.

Despite her genes and her diploma from UCLA's film school, Miranda had no desire to be an actress. She preferred working behind the scenes. But she had inherited enough talent from her illustrious parents to be able to mimic any performance she'd ever seen, a skill that had only come in handy as a party trick up until now.

All she had to do was decide which siren of the silver screen to impersonate. Would a woman-hating workaholic succumb to Rita Hayworth the way she'd looked in *Miss Sadie Thompson?* After all, that film had taken place on an island. Miranda shook her head. Sadie was too tragic. And her wardrobe was all wrong—sultry, yes, but more elegant than flashy.

Maybe she'd be Dorothy Lamour in *The Hurricane*— she did have that smashing sarong dress. But only the one. She couldn't wear the same dress for two weeks.

Miranda took a deep breath and lifted her face to the sun. The externals weren't really important, she told herself. She didn't need Hayworth's sultriness or Lamour's sarong. What she needed from her heroines was confidence. Miranda St. James couldn't talk herself into a stranger's bedroom. But Mae West and Jean Harlow could. So, she'd mimic one of the cinema sirens for a week or two.

But which one?

With an impatient shake of her head, Miranda turned her attention to the view. Maude had described San Sebastian as a tropical paradise, but she'd been a little vague about details. Miranda watched the color of the sea change from dark blue to aqua as the yacht sailed closer to the island. Mountainlike, San Sebastian jutted out of the sea, its slopes covered with blue-green foliage instead of snow. Closer to the shore, the island was a riot of color—pale pink beaches, bougainvillea in red, lavender and yellow.

The yacht anchored outside a coral reef, and the crew began taking the passengers ashore in powerboats. After a few minutes, Miranda took her place on one of the boats. From her seat in the prow, she could see that the passengers who had already reached the dock were being helped ashore by young men and women dressed in colorful Island International uniforms.

A tall man wearing a dark business suit stood on the dock, greeting the passengers as they arrived. Stuart Fordham Winslow, Miranda guessed. It had to be him. Maude had told her that Robert had personally welcomed each guest to San Sebastian. His son must be carrying on the tradition.

One of the sailors helped Miranda out of the boat and onto the dock. She fell in line behind the other passengers and in a few moments she stood in front of her stepbrother.

The moment his dark gray eyes met hers, Miranda knew she was in trouble. This was the kind of man her father had warned her about and her mother had married with shocking regularity.

Maude had said that he was good-looking, but Miranda hadn't expected him to look like the man of her dreams. She would cast him as Heathcliff in *Wuthering Heights,* or Mr. Rochester in *Jane Eyre,* any day. Stuart Winslow was wickedly handsome—tall, with black hair and steel gray eyes—but it wasn't only his looks that made him attractive. Stuart Fordham Winslow radiated an unmistakable aura of power.

He did not inspire her with sisterly feelings.

She shivered. What was wrong with her? She was supposed to cast a spell on him, not the other way around. Miranda quickly controlled her tremors and murmured, "How do you do?"

She looked up at him and gave him what she hoped would pass for a seductive smile.

He took her hand in his. "Welcome to San Sebastian, Miss ... ?"

"Miranda St. James."

Stuart continued to hold her hand as his eyes traveled slowly from the top of her silver blond head down to where her pink-tipped toes peeked out of the chrome yellow sandals that exactly matched the color of her sundress. Every place his gaze touched her sizzled like a Fourth of July sparkler.

His perusal shouldn't have bothered her. She'd been subjected to several similar once-overs on the yacht. But it did. Stuart was looking at her exactly the way Tony Curtis had looked at Marilyn Monroe in *Some Like It Hot.*

By the time his gaze returned to her eyes, she was ready for him. She held her blue eyes open wide and let a touch of vulnerability show. Her voice had just the right amount of breathlessness when she asked, "And you are?"

"Stuart Winslow, Miss St. James."

"Call me Mar—Miranda, Stuart, honey." She batted her eyes and stepped closer to him.

Stuart released her hand and took a step back. "The name is Mr. Winslow."

Miranda stuck out her lower lip. "Do we have to be so formal? I'm sure we're going to be very good friends."

"I doubt that." He motioned to one of the bellhops. "Take Miss St. James to her bungalow."

She moved next to him and hooked her arm through his. He wasn't going to get away from her that easily. "Can't you take me, sweety?" she asked breathlessly.

He looked down at her, scowling. At least he was trying to scowl—his brows were drawn together and his eyes were narrowed. But there was a suspicious twitch at the corner of his mouth.

He wasn't laughing at her, was he? Miranda lowered her gaze so he wouldn't see the doubt in her eyes. She gave herself a mental shake. It was either too late or much too soon for her to have second thoughts about her ability to carry off this pseudo-seduction.

Stuart tried to remove her arm from his, but Miranda refused to cooperate. She slowly trailed her hand down his arm, feeling the muscles bunch and tense at her touch. Aha! she thought. He wasn't completely immune to her charms.

Sure that she had his complete attention, she turned and walked away, swaying her hips provocatively. "See you later, honey."

Miranda sashayed to the end of the dock where a fleet of vehicles resembling golf carts waited. The bellhop helped Miranda into one of them. He'd obviously noticed her walk—he was goggle-eyed. She couldn't resist a quick glance over her shoulder to see what effect her sexy little stroll was having on Stuart.

None. He wasn't even looking her way. Miranda frowned. This femme fatale business was not as easy as it looked.

The cart moved away from the curb and started down a narrow roadway lined with coconut palms and bougainvillea vines. Miranda ignored the scenery and reviewed her performance. What had gone wrong? The way she'd come on to Stuart he should have followed her to the ends of the earth. He hadn't even watched her walk ten feet to the end of the dock.

Maybe she'd come on too strong.

Stuart Winslow gave every indication of being the stuffed shirt Maude had said he was. If he was an all-work-and-no-play kind of guy, maybe he didn't have time for casual flirtations. That would make her job difficult, but not impossible—not with her repertoire of sex goddesses to model herself after.

Her first step would be to discover what kind of woman appealed to him. She had time to do that—she had two whole weeks to wangle an invitation to Sugar House. So, she'd use the first few days to observe Mr. Winslow. He couldn't spend all his time in an office. That wasn't the way his father had made Island International resorts the favorite playgrounds of the rich and famous. Stuart had to mingle with the guests. And when he did, she'd be waiting for him.

Miranda curved her lips into a wicked smile. She'd hang out in the lobby and the restaurants, at the pool and on the tennis courts. She'd find out everything she needed to know about Stuart Winslow, and then she'd use Maude's tricks and a few of her own to get what she wanted—an invitation to dinner at Sugar House.

Her plan of action decided, Miranda returned her attention to her surroundings.

"Where are we going?" she asked. "The hotel is up there." She pointed to the rose-colored stucco building hugging the side of the mountain.

"You're not at the hotel, miss," said the driver as he stopped the cart. "This is your bungalow."

"Bungalow? I don't want a bungalow. Not this one, anyway. It's too far away from—" Miranda bit her lower lip. She'd been about to say too far from Stuart. "I'm sure there's been a mistake. I reserved a suite in the main hotel.''

Miranda jumped out of the cart and headed for the bungalow. ''Please wait while I call the concierge.''

# Chapter Two

Stuart found Aunt Polly hovering by the door to the executive suite when he returned to his office after greeting the resort's new guests.

Polly followed him into his office. "What's she like? Is she pretty? Did she tell you who she is? Does she look like Maude?"

"She's very pretty. She didn't say she was Maude's daughter, and she doesn't look like her." Stuart stopped in front of his desk and turned to face his aunt. "But she did remind me of someone. I haven't figured out who."

Polly's eyes glittered with curiosity. "Tell me everything."

No way. He wasn't about to tell his spinster aunt about his X-rated reaction to Miranda. She'd be shocked. Besides, he hadn't come to terms with it himself, yet. "I introduced myself. I don't think she heard me. She called me honey. And sweety."

"She didn't."

"She did." He walked behind his desk.

His aunt perched on the arm of the chair facing Stuart's desk. "What else?"

Stuart sat down. "She introduced herself. She said she was sure we were going to be very good friends. I told Joseph to take her to her bungalow and he did."

"And?"

"And nothing."

"That's all?"

"Yeah." Stuart put one elbow on the desk and rested his chin on his fist. "Except . . . something about her was familiar."

"She must look like Maude."

"A little, I guess. Miranda *is* a blonde. But her hair isn't gold like her mother's. Hers is more . . . silvery. And her eyes aren't green, they're blue. She's taller than Maude by a couple of inches—and she's not skinny."

Polly rolled her eyes. "Green! Maude Merrick's eyes are not green. She's celebrated for her turquoise eyes. And Maude is slender, willowy—not skinny."

"Whatever you call it, Miranda isn't it. She has curves like—" Stuart slapped his hand on the desk. "That's it! That's what I recognized. She's got a body like Marilyn Monroe, and her breathy kind of voice." Not to mention the sexiest walk he'd seen off the silver screen. It had taken all his self-control not to follow Miranda when she wiggled and jiggled her way off the dock.

"You don't say," murmured Polly. "She's one of your favorites, isn't she?"

"Miranda?"

"Marilyn. Do you suppose Miranda knew that?"

The phone rang before he could answer. Polly picked up the receiver and said, "Mr. Winslow's office." She listened for a few moments. "Very good. You did ex-

actly what Mr. Winslow asked you to do." She hung up.
"Miranda called to complain about her accommodations."

"I thought she might. The bungalow is kind of remote."

"Raoul's having a basket of fruit and some wine delivered to her, with apologies from the management."

"Good. Can't have the guests upset." He grinned at his aunt. "Especially not family."

Miranda took another bite of papaya.

There had to be a mistake. She was sure Maude had booked a suite in the main hotel—not a secluded bungalow on the beach.

Not that the bungalow wasn't lovely. The rattan and wicker furniture, the cushions covered in elegantly patterned chintzes, the bold primary colors all provided the perfect setting for a tropical holiday.

Miranda walked across the bare, polished terrazzo floors to the patio door and looked outside. She had a view of the lagoon from her private terrace—a terrace that overlooked a small swimming pool, artfully landscaped to resemble a jungle pond. All in all, a wonderful spot for a vacation.

But a terrible location for surveillance.

She'd made the bellhop wait while she called the concierge about moving to the main hotel. The concierge had been very polite, very concerned and very sure that the main hotel was completely filled.

She eyed the basket of fruit that had arrived at her door almost as soon as she'd hung up her phone. Island International was certainly efficient with its apologies. And its service—the woman who'd delivered the fruit had stayed long enough to unpack Miranda's new wardrobe.

The maid had ignored Miranda's protestation that she could do it herself. It appeared that guests at Island International resorts were not allowed to take care of themselves.

Miranda stifled a yawn as she swallowed the last bite of papaya and licked the juice from her lips. She'd been through goodness knew how many time zones since she'd left California a week ago, and it was beginning to catch up with her. Maybe she should call room service and make an early night of it.

No. Hiding in her room wouldn't get her closer to Stuart. She had to go to dinner at the main hotel to observe her quarry and she might as well see if a face-to-face confrontation with the concierge would turn up a forgotten suite.

Besides, she shouldn't waste the opportunity to wear one of the dinner dresses that Maude had insisted on buying for her. Mentally, she reviewed the gowns waiting on padded satin hangers in the closet. Which one should she wear tonight? She needed the perfect costume to make Stuart notice her.

Miranda was dismayed to feel her pulse quicken at the thought of seeing him again. All right, so he was attractive. Big deal. Hadn't she been around attractive men all her life? If exposure to hunks built up immunity, she should be well and truly inoculated. Even if she wasn't, Stuart was the wrong man to get feverish over.

He was the villain of the piece in Maude's scenario.

She was supposed to lure him on until she got to the safe, then spurn him. Miranda sighed. She'd have to concentrate on the spurning bit. Maude had spent most of the time preparing her for the luring part.

Miranda smiled. She could take comfort remembering that Maude had thought she could handle Stuart, and her mother *was* a consummate judge of men. Not as husbands, of course, but she knew everything about how to attract and ensnare the male of the species. And she'd taught Miranda as many of her secrets as she'd been able to in the few days they'd had together.

The wardrobe, for example. Miranda had never owned so many silk and lace garments, not to mention the sequined, feathered and gilded creations the likes of which she'd never even tried on before, much less worn. She had owned pretty clothes before, but not seductive ones. She hadn't needed them. The last two years she'd spent alone in Waldo Wisdom's private theater, in an occupation more suited to denim and cotton than silk and satin.

But now she had a dozen sexy gowns and suddenly she knew just which one to wear. She went to the closet and quickly found the dress she wanted—white silk with a short, full skirt and halter neckline. It reminded her of the dress Marilyn Monroe made famous in *The Seven Year Itch*.

After a relaxing bubble bath in the oversize marble tub, she applied her makeup according to Maude's precise instructions. When Miranda was done with paint-your-face-by-the-numbers, she slipped the dress over her head. The feel of the silky material on her creamed and powdered skin was just what she needed to get into character.

Miranda stepped into silver sandals and picked up her evening bag. Ready to stalk her prey, she left the bungalow and walked to the main hotel.

A few minutes later Miranda stared glumly at her menu.

It was the only thing to look at. The maître d' had seated her at a table in a corner of the dining room. A secluded corner, Miranda thought—one might even say cloistered. It was behind a post and screened by a huge potted palm. She couldn't see anything or anyone. Even worse, no one could see her.

Either her luck was bad or the service at San Sebastian was slipping. Besides being seated at the worst table in the restaurant, she'd struck out with the concierge. He'd been just as definite in person as he'd been on the phone. The hotel was fully booked for the next month.

A flash of movement caught her eye. The potted palm was quivering. "Hello, is there anyone there?" Miranda asked in a loud stage whisper. If there wasn't, she was talking to a plant.

"Sorry, we didn't mean to disturb you." A man appeared, a sheepish grin on his face. He tugged a pretty redhead from behind the palm.

"Please do. I was beginning to wonder if I'd ever be disturbed again. The location of this table leaves a lot to be desired." Miranda laughed.

"So you didn't ask to be seated here?" asked the man. He slanted a triumphant grin at his companion.

"Good grief, no. Who'd want to sit behind a post and a potted palm?" Light dawned. "Except a honeymoon couple?"

"Guilty. I'm Jack Richards, and this is my bride, Marie." He curved a possessive arm around his wife. "Would you mind switching tables?"

"Are you kidding? I'd love to."

Moments later, Miranda was happily ensconced at a table with a view of the entire dining room—with the exception of the table she'd just left. She was almost sure the maître d' hadn't been pleased about the switch, but he couldn't very well refuse three paying customers.

The waiter had just placed Miranda's dessert in front of her when her quarry strode into the restaurant. The

sight of Stuart dressed in evening clothes made her reach
for her spoon. She needed something soothing to slow
her racing pulse. Miranda took a bite of the mousse. It
was chocolatey, sweet and creamy smooth. Delicious.

Stuart would taste better.

Shocked, Miranda put down her spoon and stared at
the rich dessert. She'd never thought about how a man
might taste before. What was wrong with her?

She was frustrated. That had to be it. Well, who
wouldn't be, after two years as a celibate mushroom?
She'd spent months alone in the dark, watching other
people make love. No wonder she was reacting to Stuart
like a flower responding to the sun. She had to remember that she was only *pretending* to be attracted to Stuart.

Miranda gave herself a mental shake and looked up
just as the maître d' rushed to Stuart's side, his hands
held palm out in front of him. He spoke rapidly and
Stuart tilted his head to listen. The man said something
that made Stuart jerk his head up and look directly at her.

With effort, Miranda pulled her thoughts back to her
role. She gave Stuart her best imitation of Marilyn Monroe's innocently seductive smile and took another bite of
chocolate mousse. He nodded coolly and turned away
from her. He began working the room and Miranda settled back to watch.

Stuart did not intrude upon the diners unless they
made the first move. If invited, he'd stop at a table for a
brief conversation, then move on. Miranda noticed that
he listened more than he talked. She liked the way he
tilted his head and paid close attention to the person
speaking to him.

Except when the person was a beautiful woman. She
didn't like that at all. Which was ridiculous. She was
supposed to be finding out what kind of woman ap-

pealed to him. All women, it appeared. Young, old. Blonde, brunette. He had a smile for them all.

He was getting closer. Miranda felt herself quivering with anticipation. As he approached her table, she tossed her head gently, just enough to make her hair swirl enticingly around her shoulders. She used the tip of her tongue to lick the last trace of chocolate mousse from her lips.

Stuart walked by her table without even a glance in her direction.

Shocked again, Miranda quickly signaled her waiter for the check. Why, out of all the women in the room, had he passed her by?

The waiter presented the check, and she scrawled her name across the bottom and got up. Stuart was several tables away, talking to a suavely handsome man.

As she walked by the table, the man stood and said, "I was just asking Winslow here for an introduction. Those of us vacationing alone should—"

"Miranda St. James, Carter Daigle," said Stuart ungraciously. He walked away.

The man's eyebrows shot up. "Strange. Never known Winslow to be rude. Must be the strain of dealing with those takeover rumors. Ah, well, that's his problem. My problem is loneliness and you, beautiful lady, can solve it by joining me for coffee."

"I'm sorry, not tonight. I need to talk to Mr. Winslow."

She left Mr. Daigle with a brilliant smile—the way he'd ogled her bolstered her sagging self-confidence—and hurried after Stuart. He had left the dining room and was halfway across the lobby when Miranda caught up with him.

"Good evening, Stuart."

"Miss St. James."

"Nice place you have here."

"Thank you." His gaze swept the lobby.

"My dinner was delicious."

"Good." Stuart looked at the front desk.

"The service was impeccable."

"Naturally." He turned his attention to the bell captain's station.

"There is one tiny little problem . . ."

"Oh?" He nodded to the concierge.

"My bungalow. I'm miles from the hotel." He looked at her. About time, she thought. It was hard to vamp a man who wouldn't even look at you.

"Not miles. The resort's not that big. One mile maybe."

"Through the jungle." She shuddered delicately.

"The grounds are quite safe, Miss St. James. Now, if you'll excuse me—"

He started to walk away. Miranda panicked and grabbed his arm. "No. Wait. I want a room here, in the main hotel." Her voice was squeaky, not breathless. She bit her lip, dismayed. She had to stay in character. She would never attract Stuart's interest as herself.

Stuart took her hand off his arm. "See the concierge," he said and kept walking.

"I did that already." Miranda followed him, almost running to keep up. "He said the hotel is full," she panted. At least she was breathless again.

Stuart stopped and Miranda skidded to a halt beside him. He looked at her again, frowning. "Well, then, there's nothing I can do." His expression became hopeful. "Unless you'd like to transfer your reservation to another Island International resort. Perhaps you'd prefer the main hotel at Runaway Bay?"

"No." She shook her head.

"Martha's Vineyard? Key West?"

"Never mind. I'll stay in the bungalow, for now."

She touched his arm and looked up at him, her eyes wide. "But would you please walk me home? I'm afraid of the dark." She made her chin tremble ever so slightly. He couldn't resist that, could he?

"There's no need to walk. The bell captain will arrange for you to be driven to the bungalow."

"In one of those little electric carts?"

Stuart nodded and moved away from her.

"But I want to walk." She trailed behind. At least he wasn't walking away quite so fast this time. "It's such a beautiful night."

"Then walk. It's perfectly safe."

"Maybe I don't want to be safe. Maybe I'm feeling just a little bit reckless."

Stuart stopped again. Miranda bumped into him, her breasts flattening against his back. He groaned.

"Sorry. Did I hurt you?"

He spun around and grabbed her shoulders. She looked at him, startled.

"No, you did not hurt me, Miss St. James," he said through clenched teeth. She saw the quicksilver flash in his gray eyes. Was that irritation or something else? It was gone before she could tell.

Stuart turned her around so that she was facing the hotel's main entrance. He gave her a gentle push. "Come on, let's go."

"You're going to walk me home?"

"That's what you want, isn't it?"

"Yes, but—"

"At San Sebastian, we aim to please."

He strode past her, out the door and onto the wide terrace and down the stairs. Several paths led from the hotel to various attractions—tennis courts, golf course, beach. Stuart headed straight for the path that led to her bungalow.

"Wait! I had a leisurely stroll in mind, not a foot-race."

He slowed down and looked over his shoulder. "Sorry."

He stopped and waited for her to catch up.

Miranda slid her arm through his and smiled at him.

"You're forgiven." She looked around. "It's such a beautiful night, I'd forgive you anything."

"Anything?" His eyes narrowed as he looked at her. "What did you have in mind?"

"Mmm, I don't know. Maybe a kiss in the moon-light," she said, slanting a provocative gaze at him.

"I'm walking you home. Don't press your luck."

He was provoked, all right. But not the way she'd intended. He sounded angry. Why walking her home should make him mad she didn't know, but she'd better do something to soothe the savage beast.

"Humph. You could at least pretend." Miranda leaned into Stuart, pressing the side of her breast against his upper arm

"Pretend?"

"That I'm the woman of your dreams. That we're shipwrecked on a desert island." She tugged on his arm until he stopped walking and looked at her. "That you want to kiss me."

"You have quite a vivid imagination, Miss St. James."

"Don't you? Have an imagination? You must, or you couldn't have created this grown-up fantasy."

"I didn't create this. My father did, before he died. I only inherited what he built." His voice was gruff and his eyes bleak.

"Oh, I'm sorry." Miranda touched his arm. "You must miss him."

Stuart's jaw tightened, but he didn't respond.

Tilting up her chin, Miranda persisted. "Well, your father was a dreamer. You must have inherited some of his dreams, along with the business. Tell me about him."

"He was a businessman. He built a business." His muscles tensed under her hand.

"And?" she prompted.

"He almost lost it."

"How?" Carter Daigle's words popped into her head. "Some kind of takeover?"

Stuart's laugh was harsh. "You could say that. He had a weakness for the wrong kind of woman."

"What kind is that?"

"Your kind," he said. "Beautiful and sexy."

"Thank you." Miranda smiled. Her imitation sex goddess must be on target if he thought she was beautiful. Her smile faded when she remembered what else he'd said. "So your father liked beautiful, sexy women. What's wrong with that?"

Stuart turned to face her. "He married two of them. They were expensive mistakes."

Miranda narrowed her eyes. Maybe Maude was right. Maybe Stuart did need to be taught a lesson about women—especially Merrick women. "Expensive? What do you mean?"

"They wanted more than love from my father. They almost cost him his business, too."

"You mean all this?" She waved her arm to take in the island.

"This and more. My father started with nothing—he was a merchant seaman. He started Island International with a rundown hotel in Montego Bay he won in a poker game. From that small beginning he built an empire. His wives tried to take it away from him."

"Didn't they help with the building? If they did, surely they deserved a share of the company."

Stuart shrugged. "That's what my father thought."

"But you don't agree?"

"No. I think a man's a fool to lose control of his business because of a woman."

"Being in control is important to you."

"Of course."

"And beautiful, sexy women make you lose control?"

"Not me. I'm in control."

"Of the resort?"

"Of the island. I own San Sebastian."

"The whole island?"

"Yes, Miranda, the whole island—and everything on it—is mine."

"Everything?" He couldn't mean Maude's jewelry, could he? Of course not—he didn't know about the jewels. Reassured, Miranda linked her arm in his as they walked on. "Tell me how you came to own an island."

"My father bought it from the English owners. I inherited it when he died."

"I wonder if they miss it."

"The English owners?"

When Miranda nodded, he continued, "I don't think so—they'd never set foot on San Sebastian."

Confused, Miranda stopped and looked at him. "I don't understand. Why not?"

"I don't know. Maybe it seemed too remote. They inherited the island from the descendant of a second son who came to the Caribbean to make his fortune as a sugar planter."

"How romantic. Did he make his fortune?"

"No. He returned to England a failure. The island wasn't suitable for a plantation—it didn't have a dependable supply of fresh water. San Sebastian had been deserted for nearly a century when my father bought it from his heirs."

"How sad that all this beauty was wasted for a hundred years." Miranda's gaze drifted over the swaying palms and the moonlit lagoon. "Why was it abandoned for so long?"

"Dad was the only one to see it as the perfect place for an Island International resort. The other shareholder fought him every step of the way."

"He won the battle, obviously."

"My father always won a fair fight." Stuart's eyes glittered like silver. "He also solved the water problem."

"He did? How?"

"There's a desalinization plant on the other side of the island—close to the village where the staff live."

"Aren't those terribly expensive?"

"Yes." Stuart put his hand on the small of her back and steered her down the moonlit path. "Caused quite a cash-flow problem for several years."

"But not anymore?"

Stuart stopped again. She was pleased to see that he was finally grinning. "No, not anymore. My cash flow will be just fine in a matter of months."

He took her by the hand. "Come on, let's get this stroll over with. I've got things to do."

Miranda let him pull her down the path. Stuart obviously had decided she had an ulterior motive for pursuing him. Which she did, she admitted, but not the one he thought. She wasn't after his money. All she wanted was her mother's jewels.

Well, not all. She also wanted a little adventure, a touch of romance. Stuart wouldn't mind a few kisses in the moonlight, a dance or two, would he? A harmless flirtation was just what she needed to soothe the sting from the fiasco with Daniel Eberhart.

"Stuart." He'd sped up again and she was having trouble keeping up. She tugged his hand. "Wait."

She had to make him slow down or she'd never reach her goals. Maude had told her not to be too aggressive. She was supposed to flirt only enough to give Stuart the idea, then let him take over the seduction. Or as Maude had said, "Bait the hook, but let him think going fishing was his idea."

Unless she did something fast, this fisherman was going to throw her back, not reel her in.

"Slow down," she gasped.

When he checked his pace, she pretended to stumble and launched herself at his midsection. When she hit her target, Stuart's arms came around her. It might have been only reflex, but once he had her, he didn't let her go. Miranda buried her face in his shoulder to hide her triumphant grin.

Then she coiled her arms around his neck and looked up at him, batting her eyelashes. "Sorry," she murmured seductively. "I tripped."

Stuart eyed her suspiciously. "On what? The path is as smooth as glass."

"You were walking so fast...I must have tripped over my own foot."

Stuart unwrapped her arms from around his neck. "We'd better get going."

Before he could completely disentangle himself from her clutches, Miranda moaned, "My ankle." She swayed, and Stuart's arms came around her waist again.

"Is anything wrong? Did you twist your ankle?"

She stepped on her right foot, as if testing it. "No, nothing's wrong." Before he could get away again, she leaned against his chest, pinning him against a convenient palm tree. "Look around you. What do you see?"

Stuart quickly scanned their surroundings, turning his gaze from the path to the white sands visible through the trees. "I see my island. I've seen it before."

"Look at me, Stuart. You haven't seen me before." She put her hands on his chest. He put his hands on top of hers.

"What are you up to, Miranda?"

She slid her hands out from under his and inside his jacket. "Now about being in control," she purred.

"You just don't know when to quit, do you?" he growled at her as he leaned against the trunk of the palm tree.

"Quit? We haven't even started." She moved her hands up his chest to his neck. Stuart frowned, but he put his hands on her waist.

A familiar feeling began whirring through her nerve endings. She'd felt something like it the first time she'd seen Clark Gable stand at the bottom of the staircase at Twelve Oaks with that rakish grin on his face.

Except this feeling was more intense because the man standing in front of her was real. She could see him, smell him, touch him. Stuart was not an unattainable idol on a movie screen.

Miranda used the tip of her tongue to wet her lips. Letting her eyes flutter shut, she tilted her head back. Stuart groaned deep in his throat, and she felt his warm breath on her mouth. His lips would fit hers perfectly, she knew. She could almost taste his hot, hungry mouth moving on hers. Now, she implored silently. Kiss me now!

Stuart groaned again. Had any woman ever looked more kissable? She was leaning against him now, her soft breasts pressed against his chest. He could feel her hands scorching his body as they caressed his shoulders and the nape of his neck before creeping upward to tangle in his hair.

He wanted to kiss her. He wanted to crush her velvet lips beneath his, wanted to plunge his tongue into the moist interior of her mouth. He wanted to wrap his arms around her slender waist and pull her even closer.

He wanted her.

Stuart jerked his head upright. He'd almost done it. He stared at Miranda, her head tilted back, her silver-gold hair shimmering in the moonlight. He'd almost lost control over Maude Merrick's daughter!

He pushed her away.

He wasn't about to follow in his father's footsteps.

# Chapter Three

Miranda slowly opened her eyes and stretched. She blinked, coming fully awake when she realized she wasn't in her room in Tynan's Beverly Hills mansion or Maude's Fifth Avenue apartment.

She was on a romantic Caribbean island and the owner wanted nothing to do with her. Her cheeks grew warm as she remembered how easily Stuart had thwarted her attempt to seduce him.

Pulling the sheet over her head, she groaned. She had never been so humiliated in all her life.

All right, so she was a little out of practice. But she knew how to get a man to kiss her. With the sex goddess of Broadway and the hunk of Hollywood for parents, she'd have to know that. It was in her genes.

So why hadn't Stuart kissed her?

Frowning, Miranda sat up and hugged her knees to her chest. Stuart might not have found her appealing, but what kind of man didn't want to kiss Marilyn Monroe? Stuart wasn't gay. Maude would have noticed.

Miranda sighed. She'd given Stuart some pretty potent cues, and he'd ignored them. She, on the other hand, had reacted to everything. To the moonlight, the soft breezes, the unfamiliar sounds and smells of the island. To him. If he'd kissed her, she'd have melted like the wicked witch in *The Wizard of Oz.*

Miranda rested her forehead on her knees.

Maybe she'd picked the wrong actress to mimic. She'd always thought Marilyn Monroe had a universal appeal, but she hadn't curled Mr. Winslow's toes. Could it be that her mimicry wasn't good enough? Granted, she'd never put her small talent to this kind of test before, but she'd always gotten rave reviews from friends and relations for her imitations.

So, if her mimicry wasn't at fault, it had to be who she'd picked to imitate. She could fix that. All she had to do was discover who Stuart dreamed about, then become his fantasy. Miranda snapped her fingers and tossed her head.

"Piece of cake."

Her stomach growled. She shouldn't have mentioned food. Resolutely, she threw back the covers and got up.

As she washed her face and put on her makeup, her thoughts remained on Stuart. What kind of woman would appeal to him? Maybe he preferred another type, someone tougher, more independent. He was certainly man enough to handle a strong woman.

She paused, powder puff poised in midair. Had she been too passive last night? Maybe she shouldn't have waited for him to kiss her. She should have grabbed him by the lapels and kissed him senseless. Goose bumps appeared on her arms as the thought of passionately kissing Stuart Winslow made her shiver. And she was on a tropical island.

Miranda brushed the excess powder from her chin and looked at herself in the mirror. Using a stronger role model wouldn't do her any harm, either, she decided. Imitating Ms. Monroe's fragile vulnerability was not protecting her from Stuart's potent charms. From now on, she'd model herself after the likes of Katharine Hepburn, Bette Davis and Lauren Bacall. Those women wouldn't let a mere man, no matter how attractive, stop them from reaching their goals. She grinned and gave her reflection the thumbs-up sign.

Miranda went to the closet and flipped through her wardrobe. What did a tough woman wear? She knew Maude hadn't packed any bronze breastplates, but surely she had something appropriate. She finally settled on tan trousers and a tailored white silk shirt.

She checked her appearance in the full-length mirror. A little too prim and proper, she decided, unbuttoning two shirt buttons. "Watch out, Stuart. I'm coming to get you."

Miranda threw back her shoulders and sauntered to the telephone. She called for one of the electric carts and in minutes she was at the main hotel.

The doorman bowed and opened the door to the hotel. Miranda nodded to the man and entered the lobby. She stood in the doorway for a moment, looking for Stuart.

"There he goes!" a woman shrieked.

Miranda saw a small boy barreling toward her. Close on his heels came the concierge and several bellhops.

"Stop him!" ordered the concierge.

She knelt down and spread her arms. The boy crashed into her. "Oof."

"Let me go, lady!" He twisted and turned, but Miranda held on tight.

"Calm down, kid. I'm not going to hurt you." She gave the boy, whose age she estimated at four or five, a reassuring smile. "What's the problem?"

Before he could answer, the boy's pursuers crowded around, shouting orders and warnings.

"You caught him!"

"Don't let him loose!"

"Watch out! He tried to bite me!"

Miranda held the boy against her side with one hand. She put two fingers of the other hand in her mouth and whistled. Loudly.

Her whistle had the desired effect on the crowd— stunned silence. Even the little boy was impressed. He stopped wiggling and looked at her in awe. She patted him on the head. "Now, will someone please tell me what's going on?"

Raoul Freret, the concierge, and an attractive gray-haired woman joined the group at the door. "Ah, Miss St. James. If you will give the boy to me," said Raoul.

"Don't let them get me!" cried the little boy. He cowered behind her and wound his arms around her thighs.

"Now, Tommy, no one's going to hurt you," said the woman. "Let Miss St. James go."

"No!" he wailed and hung on tighter.

Miranda kept her arm around the boy. "Who are you?" she asked the woman. "His grandmother?"

"No, dear. I'm Polly Winslow. I work here."

Winslow? Maude hadn't mentioned any relatives, but she must be Stuart's kin. "Well, Miss Winslow, would you mind telling me why all of you are chasing Tommy? He's scared to death."

"I want my daddy!" yelled Tommy.

"Don't we all," Polly said fervently. "Your father isn't here, Tommy. You know that." She patted the boy on the shoulder and looked at Miranda. "Bill Anderson, Tommy's father, is in the hospital in Montego Bay. He was stricken with appendicitis when he and his new bride were on their way here for their honeymoon."

"But what's Tommy doing here?" Feeling him tense, she gave the little boy a reassuring squeeze.

"Cathy, Bill's new wife, couldn't cope with Tommy and an emergency appendectomy—"

"My daddy's going to die!"

Miranda knelt down and looked Tommy in the eye. "Is that why you're so upset? You're afraid your daddy's going to die?"

Tommy nodded and two large tears slid down his chubby cheeks.

Miranda hugged him. "Oh, Tommy, don't worry. People don't die from appendicitis. I didn't."

"You had your 'ppendix out?"

"Yep. When I was sixteen."

"And you didn't die?"

"Nope. Here I am, good as new."

Tommy's chin trembled. "But they cut you, don't they?"

Miranda nodded.

"Didn't that hurt?"

"Not a bit. I was asleep while the cutting and sewing were going on."

"They sewed you up?" Tommy was looking less worried by the second.

"They sure did. That didn't hurt, either, and it left a swell scar. I'll show it to you later."

"Neat! Will you teach me how to whistle, too?"

"Sure. After breakfast. I'm starved. How about you?"

"Me, too."

"Well, then, let's go to breakfast."

Miranda took Tommy by the hand and led him toward the coffee shop. Polly Winslow followed. "It's awfully nice of you to offer to have breakfast with Tommy."

"It won't be a chore. He's a little doll. But I still don't understand why he's here alone."

"Bill and Stuart are old friends. Cathy called Stuart when the emergency arose and asked him to take care of Tommy until Bill is out of the hospital—two or three more days. She was supposed to engage a nanny, but the woman she hired won't fly, so we've been trying to cope using the hotel staff. It's not working very well, as you see."

Miranda only hesitated a moment. "I wouldn't mind spending time with him. If it's all right with you. And Tommy." The seduction of Stuart Winslow would have to wait for a day or two. Tommy needed her.

"We can't let you ruin your vacation, Miss St. James."

"Call me Miranda, please. And it won't ruin anything. Tommy and I'll have a good time together, won't we, sport?"

"M-Mandy?" stuttered Tommy, shifting his wide-eyed gaze from the older woman to Miranda. "Are you going to be my nanny?"

"Miranda. But you can call me Mandy if you want, Tommy. And I'd be pleased to be your nanny."

"Okay. Let's go eat. I want pancakes. With lots of syrup. Can we go swimming after we eat?"

"If we wait an hour."

"Now, Tommy. Miranda can't stay with you all day. She has other things to do." Polly Winslow turned to Miranda and explained, "My nephew is arranging for one of the maids to spend the day with him."

"Don't want a maid! I want Mandy!"

"She's too old for you, Tommy," said a low-pitched, masculine voice. Stuart had joined the small group standing at the door to the coffee shop.

Tommy stamped his foot. "Don't care. I want her!"

At least she'd charmed one male this morning. She slanted a glance at Stuart. Judging from the scowl he was directing at her, he was still impervious to her charms. Think Lauren Bacall, she told herself. Bogie's scowls never intimidated her.

Miranda coolly raised an eyebrow and said, "I don't mind spending time with this young man. He wants me."

"She's going to show me her 'ppendix scar."

It was Stuart's turn to raise an eyebrow.

"That's right, Tommy. Maybe we could call your mother after breakfast and see how your dad is doing."

"She's not my mom. My mom died."

"Oh, I'm sorry. But now you have a second mom. We could call her, couldn't we?"

"Yeah," said Tommy, nodding his head vigorously. "Then we're going to go swimming like you said, and then we'll read a book and then—"

"Whoa, there, Tommy." Stuart held up a hand. "Miss St. James is not spending the whole day with you."

Tommy looked up at Miranda, chin trembling. "Why not?" he whispered. "Don't you like me?"

"Of course I like you. And I'll stay with you as long as you want me to. If it's okay with Stuart."

Tommy turned to Stuart, a smug look on his childish face. "See? Told you. She's going to be my nanny."

"Do you have any experience caring for children?" asked Stuart repressively.

"I think I can manage. I've seen *Mary Poppins* six or seven times," she quipped.

Stuart didn't laugh.

Miranda shrugged. "Bad joke. Child care isn't a laughing matter. Well, then, seriously—I was a certified baby-sitter when I was in high school—we had to take courses in child development and emergency first aid to get our certificates. I baby-sat for three or four years—never had any complaints."

"I guess it will be all right for you to spend the day with Tommy," Stuart said reluctantly.

Tommy tugged on her hand. "You can spend the night with me, too, Mandy. Will you read me a bedtime story?"

Spend the night? "Does Tommy have his own room at the hotel?" Miranda blurted. She hadn't thought of using the child to get to the main hotel, but—

"Hardly. He's staying with me," said Stuart.

Miranda raised an eyebrow. So Tommy was staying at Sugar House. "Really? How interesting." Sometimes virtue was its own reward. Now she had two routes to her goal. So far, Tommy was a lot easier to charm than Stuart.

"When are you going to teach me how to whistle?" asked the little boy.

"After breakfast, before swimming," she told him.

"Neat."

"You were the one who whistled?" asked Stuart. He looked impressed.

"Loud whistling is a survival skill in New York."

"Stuart never learned how to whistle," said Polly.

Stuart glared at his aunt.

Miranda took Tommy by the hand and pushed open the glass doors to the coffee shop. "Why, Mr. Winslow, whistling is easy." She looked at Stuart over her shoulder and added, "You just pucker up your lips and blow."

The door shut firmly behind her.

"Close your mouth, Stuart. You're gaping."

"Lauren Bacall—*To Have and Have Not,*" Stuart muttered.

"Beg pardon?" said Aunt Polly.

Stuart shook his head to clear it. Miranda had done it again—left him in a daze. "For some reason, that woman keeps reminding me of movie stars. Last night, Marilyn Monroe. This morning, Lauren Bacall."

"How nice for you," murmured Polly.

Stuart spun around and strode toward the concierge's desk. Polly followed.

"Have Miss St. James's things moved from the bungalow to the suite we were holding for Bill and Cathy Anderson." So much for keeping Miranda isolated and away from him. He needed her close by—because of Tommy, of course.

"Miss St. James has kindly offered to look after Tommy for the next day or two," Polly explained to the bewildered Raoul. "It will be more convenient if she's in the main hotel."

"Kindness has nothing to do with it," Stuart grumbled. "She's using Tommy to get close to me."

"Oh, no. Do you really think so?" asked Polly.

"Does she look like a nanny to you?" Stuart took Polly by the arm and steered her toward the elevator to the executive suite. "I want to know where they are every minute. See to it."

"Please," Polly added.

"Yeah, please. Sorry, Polly. It's been a rough morning. I lost control there for a minute." He ignored Polly's startled look. He knew what she was thinking—he never lost control. "Keep me posted on where they are and what they're doing. We are responsible for Tommy's care, after all."

"I'll take care of it," said Polly.

Several hours later, Stuart put down the quarterly financial statement he'd been staring at with unseeing eyes and buzzed for Polly.

As soon as she came through the door he asked, "Where are they?"

"On the beach at the cove near Miranda's bungalow—Miranda's *former* bungalow."

"The boy's all right?"

"She hasn't crowned him yet, if that's what you mean."

"Sarcasm, Aunt Polly?"

"I think you're being unfair to Miranda. She's doing a very nice thing."

"For her own reasons. She wants to get close to me."

"Spending time with Tommy isn't getting close to you."

"She's in the main hotel now, not in an isolated bungalow."

"She didn't ask to be moved. That was your idea."

"I know. I don't want to argue about it, Polly." He got up. "I think I'll take a break."

"In the middle of the day? What about your list of things to do?"

"I'll do them tomorrow." He walked out, leaving his aunt standing in the middle of his office with her mouth hanging open. He'd shocked her for the second time that day. He never put off until tomorrow...

A few minutes later Stuart walked out of the owner's suite. He'd exchanged his dress-for-success blue suit for shorts and a colorful Hawaiian shirt Polly had bought him for his thirtieth birthday two years ago. He hadn't gotten around to wearing it before.

He headed straight for the beach where Miranda was taking care of Tommy. He told himself it was concern for the boy's safety that had driven him out of his office. Bill and Cathy would expect him to keep an eye on whoever was looking after Tommy. That was the only reason he was headed for the beach. What else could it be? Certainly not that he wanted to see Miranda again. No, Tommy was definitely his only concern. Miranda was probably sunning her spectacular body and letting the boy run wild.

He stopped beneath the shelter of the palm trees that fringed the secluded cove and took in the scene on the beach. Miranda was sitting cross-legged on the sand next to Tommy. They were building an elaborate castle complete with turrets, battlements and a moat.

"My stepmother doesn't love me." Tommy's voice carried to where Stuart stood.

"What makes you think that?"

"She sent me away."

"She probably wanted to stay at the hospital with your dad."

"I wanted to stay, too."

"I know you did, but I'm sure she thought you'd be better off here. There isn't much to do in a hospital except sit around and wait. She sent you somewhere you could have fun—she must love you a little."

Tommy stuck out his lower lip. "No, she doesn't."

"That's too bad." Miranda showed Tommy how to use a shell to cut out notches in the top of a castle wall. "How many people do love you, do you suppose?"

Tommy put down his shell and furrowed his brow. "Dad does. Dads hafta love ya. Grandma Rose and Grandpa Tom—I'm named after him. Aunt Mary. Granny and Papa Anderson. Unca Stuart and Aunt Polly."

"Lots of people love you."

"Yeah, I guess."

"Well, then, there's nothing to worry about."

Tommy looked at her, still frowning. "Why not?"

"Because you're loved by lots of people. You can add me to the list."

"I can?"

"You sure can. You stole my heart in about a minute and a half."

Tommy climbed into Miranda's lap. "I did?"

"Yes, you did, you little charmer. So don't worry about your stepmother. She's probably nervous about being a stepmom. It's not easy, you know."

"Stepmothers are wicked. In stories."

"Now, Tommy, you can't blame Cathy for what happened to Cinderella and Snow White. I bet if you give her half a chance, she'll love you to pieces."

"What if she doesn't?"

"I guess you'll have to get by with all us other people loving you." She gave him a hug and gently pushed him off her lap. "Get back to work, now. We have to finish the north tower before the tide comes in."

Tommy jumped out of her lap and picked up his pail and shovel. Stuart left the trees and walked onto the beach.

"Hi!" said Tommy.

"Hello, Tommy." He spoke to the boy, but he couldn't keep his eyes off Miranda. The red bikini she was wearing wasn't as revealing as some he'd seen, but hers exposed enough sexy curves and silky skin to make his mouth dry. "You do have a scar." Only a sliver of a scar, barely visible on the pale skin of her abdomen.

She covered the inch-long scar with her hand. "Why would I lie about something like that?" she challenged.

"Why would you lie about anything?"

He thought she flushed, but it might have been the sun that was coaxing color into her cheeks.

"You're awfully pale for a California girl. Or are you from New York?"

"I've spent time on both coasts. How did you know where I'm from?"

"You said whistling was a survival skill in New York. You put a California address on your reservation card and, except for the pale skin, you look like a California girl, Miss St. James."

"Call me Miranda. I'm pale because of my job, which was in California. I spend a lot of time in the dark."

"I bet you do."

Miranda gave him a saucy grin.

"What do you do?" he persisted. What profession would she concoct for herself?

"I—" She looked away, then returned her gaze to him. "I work in a movie theater."

"Usherette?"

She gave a ladylike sniff. "Not exactly. I'm a film archivist."

Stuart turned his attention to Tommy. He didn't want Miranda to see how surprised he was that she'd told him the truth.

"Having fun, Tommy?"

"Yeah. Isn't this a neat castle? Guess who lives in it? Mandy. She's a princess and I'm a knight in shining armor. I'm going to rescue her."

Stuart knelt down next to Tommy. "From what?"

"Hoteliers," muttered Miranda.

"What's that?" asked Tommy.

"A kind of dragon." Miranda's eyes met Stuart's over Tommy's head. She winked at him.

"The most dangerous kind," said Stuart, feeling the blood race through his veins. She was definitely challenging him to put her in jeopardy.

"That's okay. I'll slay the hot'ler dragon with my trusty sword." Tommy jumped up and waved an imaginary sword in the air. "I'm going to look for dragons." He raced off.

"Don't go too far, and stay out of the water," Miranda called after him. She shaded her eyes and looked at Stuart. He flushed. She'd caught him in the act of ogling her body.

"Will I do?" she asked, in a low, sexy voice.

"Oh, you'll do. You'll do very well."

"I meant as a nanny."

"What else?" He looked out to sea. "I heard you talking to Tommy about his stepmother. You didn't learn that from Mary Poppins. How did you know what to say?"

"I had a stepparent or two myself. Sometimes they cared about me, sometimes they didn't. But I always knew I was loved."

"Who loved you, Miranda?"

"Mom. Dad. Like Tommy said, they have to love you."

"Not necessarily." Stuart picked up a handful of sand and let it trickle between his fingers. Had his parents loved him? He couldn't remember either of them ever saying the words. It didn't matter. Love had never been what he'd wanted.

Approval. That was what was important. For as long as he could remember, he'd wanted his father to be proud of him. As for Victoria . . . she couldn't love him and be intent on destroying Island International, the only thing he cared about. He brushed the remaining grains of sand from his hand and turned to Miranda.

"Are you catching cold?" he asked abruptly.

"No, why?"

"Last night your voice was soft and breathless. Now it's husky."

She cleared her throat. "Really? Are you sure you're not imagining things?"

"Oh, I'm imagining things, all right." He scooted closer to her. Had he finally found a weakness in her offense? She sounded the tiniest bit nervous. "Would you like to hear about the things I'm imagining?" he growled.

"No. I mean, yes. Later. Tommy . . ."

He could see her tough-girl facade slipping. She was nervous—and it was all his fault. Stuart grinned. He liked making Miranda nervous. It was the least he could do to her, after what she'd put him through last night. He sat down beside her. "Am I the hot'ler dragon you need protection from?"

She took a deep breath, calling his attention to the soft swell of her breasts. "Probably. Are you the one who put me in a lonely bungalow?"

Stuart shook his head, forcing his gaze from her chest to her eyes. They had to be the bluest blue he'd ever seen.

"No? I suppose you're not responsible for hiding me behind a potted palm?"

He shook his head again. And her lips were pink and pouty and begging to be kissed. He leaned toward her.

"I think you did."

He jerked his head up. "I didn't do anything." But he'd almost kissed her. Stick with the plan, Winslow, he told himself sternly.

"Well, if not you, who?"

"Who what?" He couldn't remember the plan. Or what she was talking about.

Miranda waved a hand in front of his eyes. "The bungalow. The potted palm, Stuart. Didn't you—"

He grabbed her hand. "Yeah, that was me."

"Why?"

She uncrossed her legs and knelt in the sand facing him. Her knees were almost touching his. Stuart rocked back on his heels and let go of her hand. "Maybe I was trying to keep you to myself."

She shook her head. "I don't believe you."

"Why not?"

"Because when you had me to yourself, you didn't kiss me."

"I'm shy." That was the plan! Keep her away.

"I'm not." She grabbed him by the soft lapels of his shirt and pulled his head down. Her lips had almost reached his before he remembered. It would be a fake kiss. She didn't really want to kiss him. She was seducing him to get to Maude's jewels. Stuart pulled his head up in the nick of time. Her mouth missed his and his chin caught the tip of her nose.

"Ouch!" She sat back in the sand, her hands on her nose, her eyes watering. "That smarts."

"Sorry." He hadn't meant to hurt her.

She took her hands away from her nose and grabbed his lapels again. "Kiss it and make it better," she crooned.

Stuart groaned. The shameless hussy wasn't going to give up. He put his hands over hers. He'd pry her loose and then—

"Yuck! Mushy stuff."

Miranda jerked out of his arms. "Tommy! Hi. Did you find any good shells?"

Saved by a five-year-old! Stuart sighed in relief.

Not that he'd been in any real danger, he told himself. But when had he put his arms around her?

"Nah." Tommy wiggled in between them and flopped down on the sand. "What are we going to do now?"

Miranda pulled Tommy onto her lap. She kissed him on his chubby cheek. Stuart felt mildly annoyed. That should have been his kiss.

"I don't know, sport. What do you want to do?"

"Watch cartoons on TV." Tommy looked at Stuart.

"You know we don't have television on San Sebastian," Stuart told him.

"Play video games."

"We don't have an arcade, either." Tommy knew that, too. What was the kid trying to do? Make him look bad in front of Miranda?

"Any swings, slides, merry-go-rounds?" she asked.

"No." Exasperated, Stuart shoved his hand into his hair. "Look, this resort was designed for honeymooners and empty nesters, not families with children."

Tommy squirmed around until he was lying in Miranda's arms, looking up at her. "What's empty nesters?" He yawned.

"People whose children are grown-ups," Miranda explained. She kissed the lucky kid again, this time on the forehead. "Why did Bill and Cathy plan their honeymoon here, if they were going to bring Tommy along?"

Stuart swallowed another groan and ruthlessly squelched a craving to change places with Tommy. He wasn't falling under Miranda's spell again. "I'm not sure. I didn't think a kid belonged on a honeymoon at all, but Bill said it was a time for them to become a family."

"I think what we should do next is take a nap," Miranda said, looking right at him.

A moan escaped Stuart's lips. He knew she was talking to Tommy, but he couldn't quash the picture his libido obligingly projected. He could see himself lying next to Miranda, being cuddled and stroked the way she was cuddling and stroking the child on her lap.

"I'm not sleepy," sighed Tommy, his eyes fluttering closed.

"Of course not," she agreed. "But I am." She stood up, cradling Tommy in her arms. "Come on, tiger. My bungalow's not too far from here. You can read me a bedtime story."

"Let me carry him. And you're not in the bungalow anymore. I had you moved to a suite in the main hotel."

"I thought the hotel was full."

"We were holding a suite for Bill and Cathy. There will be another one available by the time they get here. In the meantime, if you're serious about this nanny stuff, I'll move Tommy's things in with you."

"I'm serious." Miranda smiled at him and let him take the drowsy child from her. He waited while she wrapped a red and gold skirt around her waist and gathered up Tommy's pail and shovel. They walked away from the beach side by side.

"You didn't grow up here, did you?" Miranda asked.

"No. San Sebastian has only been open five years. We lived at the resort on Martha's Vineyard when I was a kid."

"Did they have a playground there?"

"No. That resort's not meant for the family trade, either."

"Who did you play with?"

"Play?"

She looked exasperated. "Play. You know—build castles, throw balls, shoot bad guys."

"Kill dragons?"

"Exactly."

"I don't remember." There was nothing wrong with his memory, or his childhood. So what if he hadn't had any kids his age to play with? She didn't need to know that—she'd only use it against him somehow.

"What do you remember about your childhood?"

"Working. Dad started me young—helping out in the kitchen, bellboy, whatever needed doing that I was capable of handling."

"Child labor?" Miranda gave him a pitying look.

"Dad had his reasons. He didn't want me to grow up like a rich man's son, taking all this for granted. He wanted me to learn the value of work, pride in a job well done. Not bad lessons."

"No, but all work and no play..."

They reached the cart he'd left in front of the bungalow. Stuart let Miranda get in first and put Tommy in her lap. He was sound asleep. Stuart used the boy's slumber as an excuse not to talk to Miranda on the trip to the hotel.

Talking to her was a mistake. Being close to her was a bigger mistake. Miranda was no damsel in danger from dragons. Or hoteliers. She was a definite threat to one hotelier. Him. If she found out he'd taken her mother's jewels and used them for collateral, he'd be in a lot of trouble.

Not that he'd go to jail. He was the law on San Sebastian, after all. But if he had to return Maude's jewels, Monarch Hotels would know he was in financial difficulty, the bank could foreclose on the loan—he'd risk losing everything. He slanted a look at her. She wasn't worth that. No woman was.

Stuart dropped Miranda off at the entrance to the hotel, signaling for a bellhop to help her with Tommy. It wasn't cowardice that kept him from offering to escort Miranda to her suite, he assured himself. He wasn't afraid of her. He knew who she was and what she was after, and that knowledge would keep him in control of the situation.

Yeah, sure it would, he sneered. Then why couldn't he stay away from her? When he and Polly had talked about how to handle the problem of Miranda, he'd thought staying away from her would be easy. Stuart shoved his hands in his pockets. Keeping his distance from the sexy little blonde was anything but easy.

He narrowed his eyes. Had he contributed to the problem? Was she all the more tempting because he'd made her forbidden?

It didn't matter, he decided as he pulled the cart into the lot and slammed on the brakes. He'd resist her. All he had to do was remember she hadn't come to San Sebastian for him. She wasn't looking for romance. And neither was he.

Taking the elevator to his office, he resolved to forget about Miranda and get back to business. He'd wasted enough time for one day.

"Did you have a nice afternoon?" Polly asked blandly when he entered the executive suite.

He stared at her blankly, momentarily distracted by visions of Miranda and Tommy building castles in the sand. Those two had been having a wonderful afternoon. Had he ever been that carefree as a child? He didn't think so. Hell, he hadn't had much fun since he'd grown up—fun had never been one of his priorities. Until he met Miranda.

"Stuart? Is anything wrong?"

He shook his head and snapped out an order as he continued past Polly's desk. "Order some playground equipment."

"What?" She got up and followed him into his office.

"Swings, slides, that kind of thing." Stuart walked to the window and stared out. He didn't want to look at Polly. She'd see too much.

"Why?"

"There's nothing for children to do here."

"We get a child as a guest once in a blue moon, Stuart."

"I know that. And when we do, there's nowhere for them to play."

"We have swimming pools, beaches. Movies on the weekends."

"Adult movies."

"For adult guests."

"Yeah." He turned and met his aunt's gaze. She looked bewildered. He knew the feeling. And the cause.

Stuart strode to his desk and reached for the phone. "Miranda, Stuart here. Do you think Tommy would like to see *Treasure Island* tonight?" He paused. "Great. I'll arrange a private showing for after dinner. Seven? See you then." He hung up.

"You're taking them to the movies tonight?" his aunt asked.

"Yes. Call the theater and arrange it, will you?

"But I thought you wanted to stay away from her."

"There's been a change in plans."

## Chapter Four

"And they lived happily ever after."

Miranda closed the picture book and looked down at Tommy from her seat on the edge of the bed. The little boy snuggled close to her side. He yawned and closed his eyes.

"G'night, Mandy."

"Good night, Tommy." She got up and tucked the sheet around him.

Tommy sighed sleepily. "Night, Unca Stuart."

"Night, Tommy."

Even though she hadn't looked at him since she began the bedtime ritual, Miranda had been aware of Stuart leaning against the bedpost at the foot of the bed.

She'd been surprised and a little disgruntled when he'd insisted on staying to watch her put Tommy to bed. You'd think the man had never heard a bedtime story before. Miranda fussed with the covers and frowned.

Maybe he hadn't. From what he'd told her, he hadn't had much of a childhood.

Well, it didn't matter to her if he'd been a lonely little boy, she told herself firmly. There was no need for her to feel sorry for him. Stuart was all grown up now, and if he was still alone, it had to be his choice. He certainly didn't need her to keep him company.

She gave the covers one last pat, leaned over and kissed Tommy on the forehead. She straightened and walked toward Stuart, who continued to stare at Tommy with an expression that might have been wistful.

Wistful, ha! He was bored, not wistful. A wistful man was a vulnerable man. She could like a vulnerable man and she didn't want to like Stuart. That wouldn't be smart. If she liked him, she'd couldn't keep telling him lies.

"Nice kid," he said.

Miranda put her finger to her lips. "Sh. Let's go into the other room."

Obediently, Stuart followed her out of the bedroom. Miranda walked to the suite door, intending to usher Stuart out and on his way.

Stuart stopped in the middle of the living room. "Trying to get rid of me?"

"Of course not," she lied. "I just thought..." He'd be as tired as she was, she finished silently. But he hadn't spent the whole day with Tommy. She had. She'd thought about exercising the past two years, but she hadn't actually managed a trip to the gym. A day with a five-year-old had showed her just how out of shape she was.

After a very short nap, Tommy had insisted on a second swim, in the hotel pool. That had been followed by a boisterous game of tag among the palm trees. She hadn't even had time to catch her breath over dinner. The meal had been punctuated by practice whistles. After the meal, she'd helped Tommy bathe and dress for the movie. By the time she'd gotten him ready, she'd had only minutes to spend on herself.

Maude would have been appalled at the way she'd looked when Stuart arrived to take her and Tommy to the theater. Miranda had twisted her hair into a precarious topknot and she'd only had time to reapply mascara and lip gloss. After a day at the beach and in the pool, the rest of her makeup had long since disappeared.

She'd tried telling herself that the healthy glow she'd gotten from the sun would do as well as blusher and foundation, but she hadn't believed it for a minute. The mirror had told the truth—the sultry seductress had disappeared along with the melted makeup.

Even her clothes had looked like something she might have worn to work—more sophisticated than jeans, of course, but casual nevertheless.

That was then. Now was worse.

She hadn't anticipated small fingers sticky from candy when she'd put on the white linen slacks and gauzy pink blouse. Miranda winced as she realized how she must look with chocolate stains on her pants and her shirttail hanging out. Not good. Awful, in fact.

So why was Stuart looking at her the way a dieter looks at a hot fudge sundae?

"You did that very well."

"What?" He wasn't going to leave, she decided. Miranda let go of the doorknob and walked to the sofa. She sank into the comfortable cushions and looked up at Stuart.

"Getting Tommy ready for bed—the bedtime story, the kiss good-night. Did you have younger brothers and sisters?"

"Sometimes," Miranda said, remembering weekends and holidays spent with various step-siblings. She hurried on before Stuart could question that indiscreet statement. "You're an only child, aren't you?"

He nodded. "How did you know?"

"You're very...self-contained. You act like you don't need anyone."

"I don't."

"Of course you do. Everyone needs someone."

"Maybe when I was Tommy's age. Not now."

*Maybe* when he was Tommy's age? Had it been so long since anyone had taken care of him? "Didn't your mother ever tuck you in?" Miranda bit her lip, wishing she could take back the question. She didn't want to hear any more sad stories about the way he grew up.

"No. She was never around at bedtime when I was Tommy's age."

"Where was she?"

He didn't answer immediately. "In the office, helping Dad." He sat down next to her on the sofa.

"You look surprised."

"I am. I'd forgotten—it's been a long time since Mother did anything useful. She stopped working about the time I went off to prep school. By then I was too old for bedtime stories."

There was a hint of sadness in his voice, and Miranda didn't realize he'd moved closer until she felt his breath tickling her neck.

"But if you want to tuck me in—"

"It was nice of you to take Tommy and me to the movies," she said primly. She wasn't up to sexy repartee. Not tonight. Tonight she couldn't seem to make the switch from sitcom mom to cinema siren, no matter how hard she tried. The show would have to go on without her tonight. "Tommy was thrilled. And it kept him from worrying about his father. Thank you."

"You're welcome." Stuart leaned back and put his arm along the sofa cushions, grazing her shoulders. "What thrills you, Miranda?"

What an opening! She'd have jumped right on it if she'd been in character. Only she wasn't. She'd been just Miranda almost all day—ever since she'd tried to kiss Stuart and had bumped noses with him instead. Miranda looked at him out of the corner of her eye. Strange that Stuart seemed much more seducible now that she wasn't imitating a celluloid seductress. She wasn't even sure she wanted to be an imitation any longer.

That was dangerous. She had to stick to her goals. Get the jewels and get out of town. She sighed. The problem was, the more time she spent with Stuart, the less she wanted to leave San Sebastian.

"Not talking?" He dropped his arm around her shoulders. His touch thrilled her. Why didn't she tell him that? Bacall would tell Bogie. She opened her mouth, but nothing came out. She was in deep trouble if his slightest touch rendered her speechless. It wasn't only his touch making chills run down her spine, it was the thought that a man like Stuart might be attracted to her—without the lures of makeup or glamorous clothes or famous parents. Without lies. She shivered.

"Cold?" He pulled her closer.

"On a tropical island?" she managed to say. "Don't be silly." The admonishment was for herself more than him. She was being downright ridiculous—she couldn't attract him. Not without help from her friends. Marilyn, Lauren! Help! she pleaded silently.

"The suite is air-conditioned, Miranda. If you're not cold, why did you shiver?"

"I don't know. Fatigue, maybe. I've had a full day. Honestly, Stuart, I'm not cold. You don't have to hold me."

"I like holding you." He gave her a squeeze.

A wave of pleasure swept through her, making her giddy. She liked being held by him, too. If only...

She stopped and pulled her thoughts back from that dangerous detour. Speculating about what might have been if she wasn't who she was, or if she were who she was but he knew who that was, or if he wasn't who he was, or if he was, if neither of them was related to Maude—she was making herself dizzy.

She had to get the conversation back on safe ground. "How did you happen to have a print of *Treasure Island?*" she asked.

"I collect old movies."

"That's odd." If she could keep him talking, maybe she could keep him at a distance. She wasn't ready to get any closer, not while she was overtired and vulnerable to his considerable charm.

"Not really. Island International has always included at least one movie theater at each resort. My father began keeping prints of the movies he liked. I just add to the collection from time to time."

"No, I meant it's a coincidence, me being a film archivist and you being a collector. There aren't all that many privately owned film libraries."

"That makes your choice of career a little impractical, doesn't it?"

"Not really. There are quite a few collections owned by universities and corporations. It's only private film collections that are rare now that most movies are available on videotape."

"Videotape is all right, I suppose. But I prefer to see my favorite films on the big screen."

"I didn't notice anything about your collection in the brochure for San Sebastian."

"That's because I don't show my old films to the public."

"Why not? I know the resort theater shows first run movies, but you know the appeal some of those old ones have. You should have a Classics Night at the theater."

"I'll give it some thought. Tomorrow. Now, I have other things on my mind." He moved suddenly, grasping Miranda by the shoulders and turning her so that they were facing one another.

"Stuart—"

"Sh," he said, pulling her into his arms.

"But Stuart—"

"Your voice is husky again."

"It is?" Of course her voice was husky. Any second now she'd lose the ability to talk at all.

"Last night it was breathless, this morning—and now—it's husky."

He'd noticed the switch. Was that good or bad? "Which do you prefer, breathless or husky?"

"I liked the voice you used to read Tommy *Goldilocks and the Three Bears*."

"That's my voice," she blurted, surprised and pleased at the same time. She tried to move out of his arms. She wanted to look into his eyes.

"That's the one I like best." He gently pushed her head down on his shoulder.

"But—" She gave up and relaxed against his chest, her arms loosely curled around his waist. Was it really possible that she might succeed where Marilyn Monroe and

Lauren Bacall had failed? The thought made her head swim, her stomach flutter.

"Why do you switch voices?" He'd discovered her blouse wasn't tucked in. Miranda relaxed even more when his warm hands began making lazy circles on her bare back. "Are you pretending to be someone you're not?"

She tensed. "I don't know what you're talking about. I don't change my voice."

"You do."

"I don't."

"Whatever you say. I don't want to argue with you. And I don't want to talk about my movie collection." He paused. "Aren't you going to ask me what I do want to do?"

"No."

He chuckled. "I'll tell you, anyway. I want to kiss you."

"I'd love to kiss ya, but I jes' washed my hair," Miranda said in a sleepy Southern drawl.

"Bette Davis."

"Right. Which movie?"

"Cabin in the Cotton."

"Year?"

"I don't remember."

"It was 1932." She yawned against his neck. "Studio?"

"That's enough movie trivia." He tilted her chin up and looked into her eyes. "You really are tired, aren't you?"

"Mm." Her eyelids fluttered shut.

"You should be tucked up in bed like Tommy. But first—"

She felt his lips gently pressed on her closed eyes, first one, then the other. "Stuart," she murmured, opening her eyes, "what are you doing?"

"I'm trying to kiss you."

"You shouldn't. Tommy's in the next room."

"Sound asleep. What's the matter, Miranda? Don't you want to kiss me any more?"

"N-no." She levered herself away from him.

"No?"

"Not tonight. Tommy—"

"Won't know anything about it. Just one little kiss?"

"I—" She could handle one little kiss, she told herself as she leaned toward him. One kiss. Then he'd leave and she and her alter egos could regroup. She closed her eyes.

Nothing happened.

Miranda opened her eyes slightly and peered at him through her lashes. "Stuart?"

"Yes?"

"I thought you wanted a kiss."

"I do."

"What are you waiting for?"

"Some cooperation. Put your arms around my neck."

She did. His muscles tensed as she moved her hands up across his chest and around his shoulders. She sighed dreamily as her fingers traced the curve of his ears before curling into his crisp black hair. She let her head fall back against his arm and parted her lips slightly. She closed her eyes and waited. And waited.

Nothing.

Her eyes snapped open. "Now what's the matter?"

"Too much light. It's not romantic." He reached around her and switched off the lamp on the table by the sofa.

Half-reclined on the sofa, with Stuart leaning over her, Miranda closed her eyes and pursed her lips in anticipation of his kiss. He moved his face closer to hers. His warm breath feathered across her cheek. "Too dark," he muttered. "Now I can't see you."

She opened her eyes. The room was filled with tropical moonlight. "Oh, for heaven's sake! I can see you just fine."

He grinned at her. A slow, sexy grin that had her pulse racing. She wasn't a bit tired anymore.

"I can see you now, too. The moonlight makes your hair look like molten silver." Stuart lifted a strand in his hand and let it fall slowly from his fingers. He framed her face with his hands, then, just as she thought he was finally going to do it, he turned his head and rested his cheek on her shoulder.

Miranda swallowed a frustrated moan. She might as well face it. Stuart had a mean streak. Why else would he be tantalizing her with talk of kisses that never materialized? Maude said to let the man take the lead, but this man was too slow.

She was through waiting. Miranda grabbed two handfuls of Stuart's polo shirt and pulled his head up. She'd show him a thing or two. People who made other people wait didn't get real kisses.

She intended to give him one quick peck, then send him on his way. But once her lips touched his Miranda forgot her intentions. She forgot her name. All her brain cells and nerve endings were concentrated on Stuart and the sensations created by his mouth moving urgently on hers. She quivered, she tingled. She was probably glowing in the dark.

Miranda was aware that one kiss was turning into many, but each kiss was so exciting, so filled with passion, she wanted more. Pretending to be a siren, a seductress had been a game, a party trick until now. Now, each touch, each sigh, each kiss, told her Stuart wanted her. It wasn't a game any longer. She truly was a desirable woman.

"Mandy?" Reluctantly, Miranda pulled her mouth away from Stuart's and turned her head. Tommy was silhouetted in the bedroom doorway, rubbing his eyes.

She eased herself out of Stuart's arms. "What is it, sweetheart?"

"Can I have a drink of water?"

The next afternoon, Miranda held tight to Tommy's hand. They were waiting for the boat carrying his parents to dock. Tommy was so excited she was afraid he'd jump in the water and swim to meet them if she let go of him.

Bill Anderson had been released from the hospital and he'd chartered a boat to bring him and his bride to San Sebastian. Stuart had called her that morning to tell her and Tommy what time the boat was arriving. Miranda glanced over her shoulder, looking for Stuart. He was supposed to be here, too.

She was apprehensive about seeing Stuart again, but she wasn't sure why. There was nothing to be afraid of. She'd finally hooked her fish. Stuart had kissed her. Again and again. And what kisses! She'd never experienced the depth of passion he'd made her feel the night before. And he'd felt passion, too. For her.

That was the problem—he'd kissed Miranda, not Marilyn Monroe or Lauren Bacall. She was supposed to be playing a role, a role she could walk away from when the play was over. She couldn't walk away from herself. If she did finish the piece playing herself, she couldn't

count on a happy ending. At some point, she'd have to
tell Stuart who she was. How would he react once he
knew she'd deceived him? *That* was what she was afraid
of.

She looked over her shoulder again. The boat was going to dock any minute now, and still no Stuart. Was he
trying to avoid her? Maybe he regretted kissing her. Just
because the kiss had curled her toes didn't mean it had
been anything special to him. He probably kissed women
all the time. Beautiful women.

Women who told him the truth.

She couldn't do that, not yet, not without breaking her
promise to her mother. A mother who prided herself on
two things—she'd never missed a performance and she'd
never broken a promise to her daughter. Maude didn't
make promises she couldn't keep.

Miranda bit her lip. Even if she was willing to break her
promise to Maude, she wasn't ready to risk telling Stuart
the truth. Stuart liked her, but he didn't know Merrick
was her middle name. Maude had said he didn't approve
of Merrick women, and that was when he only knew one
of them. She wasn't anything like Maude, not usually,
but she had been using some of Maude's patented tricks
of the sex-symbol trade. She couldn't blame Stuart if he
came to the conclusion she threw herself at every man—
every attractive, wealthy man—she met.

If she was lucky, he'd know instinctively that she was
an honest, truthful person. When she wasn't lying for her
mother. If she was really, really lucky, Stuart wouldn't
care who her parents were. Why should he? He didn't
want or need anything from Maude or Tynan. He wasn't
another Daniel Eberhart.

On the other hand, he thought Maude had cheated his father somehow. If he knew who she was, he might throw her off his island before she got the jewels.

The boat docked before she could resolve her dilemma, and she had to concentrate all her effort on keeping Tommy from leaping off the dock onto the bobbing boat deck. The gangplank was extended and a sailor helped a gorgeous brunette off the boat, just as Stuart arrived with a wheelchair.

He introduced Miranda to Cathy Anderson and handed the wheelchair to the sailor. "How's Bill?"

"Not a good patient, I'm afraid. The doctor told him to take it easy for at least a month, and he's talking about deep-sea fishing and golfing. Not to mention s-e-x."

Stuart grinned. "It is your honeymoon."

"I know, but the doctor said—"

"There's Daddy! He's really okay, just like Mandy said."

Tommy tugged free of Miranda's grasp and ran to the gangplank. The sailor was wheeling a large, blond man across the plank.

"Tommy! Be careful!" said Cathy, her voice strained. "Don't jump on Bill. You'll hurt him."

"I can stand a little hug from my son, Cathy," Bill said, grunting as Tommy landed in his lap. "Who's the pretty lady, Tommy? Obviously Stuart is not going to introduce us."

"She's Mandy, my nanny. Can we keep her? She had her 'ppendix out, too. I saw her scar. Can I see yours?"

Bill laughed and reached one hand around his son to take Miranda by the hand. "How do you do, Mandy. Need a job?"

She grinned at him. "'Fraid not. I don't have the stamina to be a full-time nanny."

"You heard the lady, sport. You were too tough on her. Guess we'll have to get along without her."

"Guess you will," said Stuart. "You can start by letting go of her."

Bill dropped Miranda's hand. "No problem, old buddy. That's how it is, hm?"

Miranda looked from Bill to Stuart in time to see Stuart's scowl melt into a sheepish grin. What was going on? He wasn't jealous, was he?

Tommy jumped off his father's lap and grabbed Miranda's hand. "Don't want to let go of her. I want Mandy!"

"Now, son, you've got me and Cathy—"

"Don't want Cathy!" Tommy's eyes filled with tears and he clutched Miranda's hand even tighter. "Mandy loves me!"

"Hold on, Tommy," said Bill. "Cathy loves you, too."

Cathy knelt down and reached out her arms. "That's right, Tommy. I do. Won't you give me a chance?"

Tommy looked up at Miranda, his eyes opened wide. "She's not a wicked stepmom, is she?"

"She doesn't look wicked to me." Miranda winked at Cathy, who was looking a trifle bewildered. "Tommy and I had a little talk about the bad reputation fairy tales give stepmothers."

"Oh, I see." Cathy wrapped her arms around Tommy and gave him a hug. "I'll try real hard not to be wicked— not ever. Okay?"

"Okay. She does love me, Mandy." He wiggled out of Cathy's arms and turned to his father. "Mandy told me Cathy would love me once she 'laxed."

Cathy shot Miranda a grateful look. "I don't know how relaxed I am, but I do love you, kid." She ruffled his hair and took him by the hand. "Tell Miranda goodbye for now. We'll see her later. Would you join us for dinner tonight?"

"Thank you, no. I have other plans." She slanted a look at Stuart.

He raised a questioning eyebrow. "Other plans?"

"I'm having dinner with you, remember?" He hadn't asked, but surely he wouldn't call her on that in front of Bill and Cathy. Not after he'd ordered Bill to let her go. She'd hooked him, and it was time to reel him in—the sooner, the better.

As soon as she had Maude's jewels safely in her possession and away from Sugar House, she could tell Stuart who she was without breaking her promise to her mother. Then they could explore whatever was happening between them without any more half-truths cluttering up the issue.

"Dining with the guests, Stuart?" asked Bill. "You never do that. Miranda must be someone special."

"Very special," Stuart agreed. "Where are we dining, Miranda? Did I say?"

"Why, yes, you did. At your place." Miranda smiled sweetly at him. He was going along with it. With any luck, she'd be in his bedroom before the night was over.

She and Stuart in his bedroom... Miranda gulped as a sexy scenario featuring the two of them floated in front of her eyes. What was she thinking of? She'd be in his bedroom alone. The R-rated scene of her and Stuart faded out as she made herself concentrate on Maude's plan.

She'd do just what her mother had told her to do—ask to visit the powder room, taking her oversize evening bag with her. Miranda grinned, remembering what Maude had said when she'd complained that the evening bag looked like a suitcase. "He's a man, he won't notice. If he does, he'll assume you've brought your toothbrush and a negligee.''

So she'd take the bag with her, open the safe, put the jewels in the bag and get out.

"Dinner at your place, huh? Better and better," said Bill. "I always knew you'd find the right woman someday, old buddy."

"We're having dinner together, not announcing our engagement," snapped Stuart.

Bill shrugged. "Let's get this show on the road. I'm ready for a nap."

Miranda got a lump in her throat watching Cathy and Tommy walk alongside the wheelchair as the sailor pushed it down the dock to the waiting cart. They looked well on the way to becoming a happy family. She blinked back tears.

Stuart stepped in front of her and put his hands on her shoulders. He moved one hand to tilt up her chin. Staring at her face, he asked, "What's wrong?"

She sniffled. "They l-look so good together—like a real family. Families are wonderful, aren't they?"

"Some are, I guess."

Miranda thought he was going to say more, but instead he took her hand. They walked to the hotel in silence.

When they reached the lobby, Stuart turned to her and asked, "Is dinner at eight o'clock all right with you?"

"Fine. How will I get there?"

"Take the elevator to the penthouse."

Shocked, her mouth dropped open. "Penthouse? But I thought you lived at Sugar House."

He shook his head. "What gave you that idea? I live in the owner's suite here in the hotel." His eyes narrowed. "How did you know about Sugar House? It's not part of the resort."

"I must have read about it." Miranda started walking toward the bank of elevators, her thoughts in turmoil. He didn't live at Sugar House! She wouldn't get Maude's jewels tonight. She wouldn't be able to tell Stuart who she was tonight—not without risking making him angry enough to kick her off San Sebastian. Her stomach knotted. How had she gotten into this mess?

"Miranda?" She jumped. He'd followed her to the elevators. She could feel him standing behind her. "Where did you read about Sugar House?"

"I'm not sure. Isn't it a colonial great house?"

"Yes. Restored and renovated. My father lived there with . . . his second wife."

"Who lives there now?"

"No one. The house is closed."

"Why don't you live there?"

"It's more convenient being here at the hotel. Besides, Sugar House is too big for one person. I may move there someday . . . when I marry." He rested his hands on her shoulders.

She didn't want to hear about his future marriage. She had to find another way to get to Maude's safe. She shrugged out from under his hands and turned to face him. "Do you have tours? I'd love to see it."

"No tours."

He wasn't looking at her the same way, she noticed. His eyes were cold. And why shouldn't they be? She was acting more interested in a house than in him. But she had to do it.

"Why not?" she asked brightly. "Lots of people are interested in colonial architecture."

"Are you sure you're not in marketing? First you come up with Classics Night, now you're pushing tours of Sugar House."

"Don't you like my ideas?"

"Some of them. I like your idea for us to have dinner tonight."

"But not for tours of Sugar House?"

"No. Island International doesn't own the great house. I do. And I don't want strangers in my home."

An elevator door opened. Polly walked out into the lobby waving a piece of paper.

"I'm sorry to bother you, but we just received a cable from Victoria. She's on her way here. She's coming by helicopter from Runaway Bay."

"Damn!" Stuart said. "Thanks, Polly. Let me know when she arrives."

Polly stepped into the elevator. "I will," she said, letting the door close.

"Who's Victoria?" Miranda asked.

He put his hand on her waist and guided her to another elevator. He was scowling. "My mother."

"You don't look happy about her visit."

"I'm not."

"Why? Don't you get along with your mother?"

"We get along fine—as long as she's somewhere else."

"Why is that?"

"She wants to run the business, too."

"Too?" The elevator door closed and Stuart hit the buttons for both her floor and for the executive offices floor. "I don't want to run your business. I just made a few suggestions."

"That's what Mother does. She makes suggestions. For instance, she suggests we sell Island International to

Monarch Hotels." The elevator door opened. "You'll have to excuse me, Miranda. I have things to do."

As soon as Stuart arrived in the executive suite, Polly asked, "What's the matter?"

"She asked me to have dinner with her."

"Oh? And are you dining together?"

"Yes, in my suite. Tonight."

"Another first."

Stuart stared at her. "What are you talking about?"

"You have been acting out of character, Stuart. Taking time off in the middle of the day. Procrastinating. Ordering playground equipment. Now you're breaking your rule against dining with guests."

"Miranda isn't the usual guest."

"Exactly what I said. She's nicer than most of them. Helpful. Kind and considerate. Pretty, too. And she likes old movies."

"She's a liar."

"You're a thief," said Polly. "I'm sorry, dear, but aren't you a pot calling the kettle black? You're not telling her the whole truth, either."

"I have a good reason. Saving Island International."

"Maybe she has a reason, too."

"She's come for her mother's property. Why should she lie about that?"

"I don't know. You and Maude didn't part on the best of terms. Maybe Maude convinced her you'd try to keep the jewels for yourself."

"Maybe. Maude is paranoid about those jewels."

"She must be. To have installed the safe secretly, not even telling Robert." Polly shook her head in disbelief. "But Stuart, if she didn't trust your father—"

"She wouldn't trust me. I get the picture. That's still no reason for Miranda not to trust me."

"It's not?" Polly looked surprised.

So was he. What did he care if Miranda trusted him or not?

"Well, then," Polly continued, "maybe she's only trying to avoid trouble getting the jewels off the island. For all she knows, you might use your authority to charge her a hefty customs fee."

"All right, all right." Stuart threw up his hands in a gesture of surrender. "Miranda may have some reason to keep her purpose here a secret. I still have to keep her away from Sugar House."

"Yes, I know. So why are you having dinner with her?"

"Dinner in the owner's suite won't get her any closer to the safe."

"It will get her closer to the owner."

Stuart narrowed his eyes. "What's your point?"

A smile tugged at the corners of Polly's mouth. "I think you like her, in spite of everything. And she likes you."

"She has to like me. The jewels are in my house."

"When I see the two of you together, I almost forget about the jewels."

"You can bet she hasn't. You should have seen her face when I told her I lived in the hotel."

"Oh, my goodness. The owner's suite. Victoria will expect to stay with you."

"Damn! I didn't think—" Stuart shoved his hands through his hair. "Mother will expect to have dinner with me, too. The last thing I need is for her to meet Miranda."

"No, you don't need a chaperone."

"What I don't need is Mother learning who Miranda is and what she's after. She's been trying for months to find out how I raised the money to outbid her for Maude's stock."

"How would Victoria find out about Miranda?" Polly asked.

"I don't know. She might recognize her name. You did. There's no telling what she knows about Maude Merrick and her daughter—she's always been curious about Dad's second wife."

"But even if Victoria realizes who Miranda is, she'll assume she's here on vacation. She doesn't know Maude left her jewels at Sugar House."

"If Mother recognizes Miranda, she'll wonder why we didn't, and why Miranda hasn't told us she's Maude's daughter. Mother will want to know what's going on, and she'll keep pestering you, me, everyone, until she finds out."

Polly nodded in agreement. "Victoria is persistent when she wants something."

"Tell me about it. I have controlling interest of the company and she's still after me to take Monarch's offer."

"I know. I'll arrange a special dinner for Victoria and me in my suite. She won't pass that up. She'll want to pump me about you."

"Good idea. But we can't keep her and Miranda apart forever."

"That won't be necessary if Victoria doesn't recognize her. And she may not. I have a feeling not many people remember that Maude has a daughter." Polly got up. "I'll make the dinner arrangements and go to meet Victoria at the dock."

Miranda was Maude Merrick's daughter, all right, Stuart told himself as he watched Polly leave the room. He'd thought that knowledge would be a talisman—protection from the spell she was weaving. It wasn't. No matter how much he wanted to deny it, the truth was he was as besotted with her as Tommy had been.

And he wanted more from her than whistling lessons and bedtime stories. He wanted her. Even mussed up and grumpy the way she'd been last night when he'd forced her to kiss him. That had been a mistake, but one he couldn't talk himself into regretting.

Miranda Merrick St. James was a liar, and no doubt a replica of her avaricious, scheming mother, and still he wanted her—more than he'd ever wanted any woman.

And all she wanted was the jewels.

# Chapter Five

"Rafferty residence."

"Hello. Agnes? Is that you? This connection's not very good. It's me, Miranda. Is Mother there?"

"Where are you? When are you coming home?"

"In a week or so. Can I speak with Maude?"

"Your mother's not here. She's in California, but she's not staying here."

Miranda paced back and forth, chewing on her bottom lip. "Where is she staying until the wedding, do you know?"

"Somewhere in Palm Springs, but she didn't say with whom. Said she wanted her privacy—as if I'd tell the tabloids where she is." The housekeeper sniffed.

"Now, Agnes, don't get upset. I don't know where she is, either, and I'm her only child. Let me talk to Dad, please."

"He's in Arizona on location. He'll be back Sunday or Monday."

"Is there a number where I can reach him?"

"No, but he calls in every day or so for messages. Shall I tell him to call you? Is anything wrong?"

"No, nothing's wrong. There's no need for Dad to call me. Just tell him I love him and I'll see him in a few days."

Miranda hung up the telephone and walked onto the balcony. So much for that idea. If she couldn't talk to Maude, she couldn't tell her about Stuart—that he didn't live in Sugar House, that he wasn't the kind of man who'd take something that didn't belong to him.

That he was the man she'd been waiting for.

Well, maybe she wouldn't have told Maude that. She wasn't completely sure about that. Not yet, although one more kiss would probably do it. Miranda sighed dreamily. Another kiss might not be necessary—one more look from those sexy silver eyes might be enough. A nervous giggle bubbled in her throat, but she caught herself before it escaped.

Stuart didn't like giggling girls, Maude had said. Or liars. That was the problem, she thought, frowning at the telephone. She wanted him to like her. Why else would she have risked letting the hotel operator place a call to Tynan's unlisted number?

She wanted to tell Stuart the truth, and to do that, she needed to talk to Maude. Her identity was her business, but the safe and the jewels were Maude's secrets. How could she tell him who she was without revealing why she'd come to San Sebastian?

The time for casually letting slip that she was Maude Merrick's daughter had long since passed. If she told him now, Stuart would certainly want to know why she hadn't said anything, earlier. He might forgive her little deception if he knew about Maude's jewels, but Miranda couldn't tell him about them without her mother's blessing.

Maude could advise her about the signals she was getting from Stuart, too. What did it mean when a man blew hot one minute, cold the next?

Miranda sighed. She wasn't going to get any help from her mother—not for a while, anyway. No matter how much she hated keeping secrets from Stuart, she'd just have to grit her teeth and do it.

She soothed her conscience by telling herself she wasn't lying—not exactly. Stuart hadn't asked her who her parents were or why she'd come to San Sebastian, and he wasn't being hurt by not knowing the whole truth.

Sighing in resignation, she decided she had no choice. She'd keep her promise to Maude, at least until she'd gotten the jewels safely out of Sugar House.

And how was she going to do that? So far she hadn't managed to get near Maude's former home, much less in and out with a load of jewelry. Miranda left the balcony and walked inside, her shoulders slumped to match her mood.

She slipped out of her robe and into the sarong dress she'd chosen to wear to dinner—black silk splashed with exotic red flowers. Straightening her shoulders, Miranda wiped the gloomy expression from her perfectly made-up face and smiled into the mirror. The imitation siren of the silver screen was back.

Maude's plan might be falling apart, but that was no reason for her daughter to do the same. She'd just have to convince Stuart to give her a private tour of Sugar House.

It was either that or burglary.

Miranda walked out of her suite and across the hall to the elevator. She got in and absently pushed the penthouse button. Burglary might be the best way to go, she mused. At least that wouldn't involve telling Stuart any more half-truths.

Tomorrow night she'd try her hand at breaking and entering. Tonight she'd forget all about Maude's melodrama and concentrate on learning more about Stuart. A shiver of anticipation slid down her spine just as the elevator doors slid open.

Stuart shrugged into his tuxedo jacket as he walked into the living room of the owner's suite. He looked at his watch. Almost eight o'clock—Miranda would be here any minute now. It hadn't taken him long to figure out what she'd do next—she only had one choice. She had to persuade him to give her a tour of the colonial great house.

He was looking forward to being persuaded by Miranda.

Stuart flicked back his cuff and looked at his watch again. Not that she'd get her way. He had the perfect excuse to avoid showing her Maude Merrick's former home—he wouldn't be around. How would she react when he told her that he'd be leaving for Jamaica first thing in the morning?

A knock sounded. He walked through the foyer and opened the door. At the sight of Miranda, his heart slammed against his ribs. He'd never seen anyone so lovely. Or so happy. Her smile made him grin in response. She looked like a woman confident of her powers of persuasion. He allowed himself a lingering inspection of her womanly curves, finding it sweet torture to look and not touch.

"I was just coming to get you," he said, moving aside as she entered the foyer.

"Am I late?" she asked.

"No, you're right on time." Unable to keep his hands off her, he put his palm on the small of her back and guided her into the living room. "I was impatient. That's why I was coming after you."

She stopped in the middle of the living room and turned to face him. "You were?" she asked, licking her lips.

Mesmerized, Stuart followed the movement of her tongue with his eyes. "If you want dinner, I'd suggest you stop that," he said, his voice husky.

"Stop what?" She looked at him, her eyes huge and innocent. She sounded cool and collected, but he saw the pulse in her throat jump erratically.

"Licking your lips." He stared at her mouth. "It makes me want to do the same."

She moved away from him. "I'm hungry."

"For?" he asked suggestively. Seducing the seductress was a lot of fun.

"Whatever you have. I never met a food I didn't like." Miranda surveyed the room. "Where are we dining?"

"On the terrace. What do you think about my home?" he asked, surprised that she seemed more interested in dinner than in him.

"It's beautifully decorated," she said politely.

"But?"

"It doesn't look like anyone's home." A tiny frown creased her forehead. "I don't think I'd like living in a hotel."

"No?"

"No. It's too impersonal—not the place to raise a family."

"You plan to raise a family?"

"Someday. Don't you?"

"Maybe," he said warily. He could be wrong about Plan B. Maybe Miranda was after more than her mother's jewels. Her very own premarital contract, for instance?

"You won't live in a hotel suite after you're married, will you?"

"Why not? My parents did."

"What if your wife wants to live in a house?"

Stuart narrowed his eyes. "Living at the hotel is convenient. And comfortable. Most women would like daily maid service. Not to mention twenty-four-hour room service."

"But surely, after you have children—"

"I lived in hotels when I was a child," he reminded her. Stuart rubbed the back of his neck. Miranda's prattling about marriage and families was making him tense. "I liked it."

"Did you?" she murmured. She looked like she didn't believe him.

"I did!" Exasperated, he shoved his hand through his hair. "It was a great way to learn the business!"

She gave him a pitying glance. "But you never learned to play."

He ushered her onto the terrace and seated her at the elegantly appointed table. If she was trying to seduce him, she was sure going about it all wrong. Making him feel defensive about his childhood, his devotion to business, harping on marriage—and not one mention of Sugar House. What was she up to?

"Did your mother arrive?" she asked, once he'd taken his place opposite her.

"Yes. But she won't be joining us. She's having dinner with Polly."

Miranda ate the exotic foods the waiter placed in front of her with obvious enjoyment, and conversed knowledgeably on a wide range of topics. She was a charming dinner companion and if she was more reserved than he'd expected, it could be due to the fact that they weren't alone with each other, yet.

The waiter removed the dinner plates and served coffee.

"Why does your mother want to sell the resorts?" asked Miranda, taking a sip of the steaming brew.

"She wants money—more than she gets from dividends."

"What for?"

"Travel, expensive clothes. Jewelry."

"Why?"

"I don't know why. Because she's a woman. More coffee?" She shook her head and Stuart signaled the waiter to clear the table.

As soon as the waiter had left them alone, Miranda said, "You seem to think all women are gold diggers."

"No, not all. But my father had a definite weakness for the type." He waited a heartbeat, then asked, "You do know that Maude Merrick was my stepmother?" Let her go on the defensive for a while!

"Oh, yes, I know everything about Maude Merrick. She's my favorite actress." She smiled at him, but her smile was a little wobbly.

He scowled at her. "Well, she's not mine. I think it was Dad's marriage to Maude that changed my mother—she wants more money so she can compete with her."

"Compete?" Miranda looked puzzled. "For what?"

"Mother wants to enjoy the life-style she imagines Dad had with that woman."

"That woman?"

Blue eyes flashed. He was definitely getting beneath her skin. Stuart hid his grin behind a napkin.

"I take it you didn't like your stepmother?" Miranda asked haughtily.

"I didn't like her taking advantage of my father." He got up and helped Miranda stand.

"How did a mere woman manage that? I thought your father was a shrewd businessman."

Stuart clenched his jaw. She was getting under his skin, too. "He was. But he wanted Maude. She made him want her."

Miranda shot him a scornful glance. "She held a gun to his head, I suppose."

He wanted to shake her. Miranda should be outraged at the way he was talking about her mother—even if everything he said was true. Instead, he was the one on the verge of a tantrum. He had to get control of himself. He couldn't afford to lose his temper as long as his plan had a chance of working. Somehow he was going to make Miranda admit who she was. "No gun. She promised him..."

"What?"

"Everything a man wants from a woman." Stuart put his arms around her waist and pulled her against him. He'd make Miranda be the one to lose control, one way or another. "Everything I want from you."

Miranda flattened her palms on his chest. "Then I'm sure your father got what he wanted. I've heard that Maude Merrick always keeps her promises."

"Oh, she fulfilled her promise. But not until he gave her—"

"His love."

"Don't be naive, Miranda. Love had nothing to do with it. Maude wanted marriage."

Miranda tilted her head and looked up at him. "And your father didn't?"

"He would have been satisfied with an affair."

"Maude Merrick doesn't believe in affairs. That's one reason she's been married so often."

"You know a lot about her."

"I read it in a magazine," she said glibly.

"The magazine article was wrong. Maude didn't avoid affairs because of her morals—she wanted money and she used marriage to get it. She divorced her husbands as soon as she'd bled them dry."

She stiffened and tried to push him away. "That's not true! All Maude's husbands left her."

He held on tight. "Not my father."

"Well, she didn't leave him, either," she pointed out.

"She didn't have time. They were married less than a year. But I don't think he would have been her last husband."

"Neither do I. Not if he didn't love her."

Stuart let her go and shoved his hands in his pockets. "I don't know if he loved her or not."

"If he didn't, he cheated her."

"No, he didn't. She got what she wanted—marriage and a very lucrative prenuptial contract."

"And all because she used her womanly wiles to make your father weak with desire?" Miranda gave a decidedly unladylike snort.

"Exactly."

"You really believe a woman can do that to a man?"

Stuart nodded, his eyes narrowed as he looked at her.

"Have you ever wanted anyone that much?"

He shook his head. "No. And I never will. No lying, scheming woman is going to make a fool out of me."

"Oh, no?" Miranda purred, stepping close and sliding her arms around his neck. "Well, you don't have to worry about me." She met his gaze steadily, blue eyes opened wide.

Miranda was the picture of sincerity. No wonder his father had succumbed to Maude's charms—she'd had years to hone her skills. Stuart was struggling mightily to resist Miranda, and she was a novice.

"Don't I?" His hands came out of his pockets and slid around her waist again. But when she tried to move toward him, he held her in place. He didn't want her to get closer.

"No, you don't."

Stuart watched as the lie fell easily from her tongue. "You don't want anything from me?" he asked.

She reached up to stroke the line of his jaw. "I didn't say that."

"What do you want?"

"Not your money." She used her forefinger to trace his bottom lip.

"No? What then?" He tightened his hold on her waist. "Tell me, Miranda."

"You," she whispered breathlessly. "I want you."

"Good." It was about time she admitted that. Stuart turned her around and pushed her toward the door. "Let's go to your suite."

Miranda dug her heels into the lush carpet and refused to budge. "What for?"

He smiled grimly—her professed desire for him hadn't lasted long.

"My mother's staying with me. We can't make love here."

"Make love?"

He stopped pushing her toward the door. "You said you wanted me," he breathed in her ear. "Didn't you mean it?"

She looked at him over her shoulder. "Yes. But I didn't mean... That is, we can't..."

Stuart stopped, crossed his arms over his chest and leaned against the wall. "You lied to me."

"No. Not about that. I do want you." She turned. His disbelief must have shown on his face. "I do!" she insisted. "But that doesn't mean I want an affair."

"I see. You want me, but you don't want an affair." He gave her a sardonic smile. "This is beginning to sound familiar. I suppose you won't settle for anything less than a ring on your finger before—"

She put her hands on her hips. "You have a problem with that?"

"It's a little soon to be talking of marriage."

"We weren't talking about marriage. You were trying to hustle me off to bed."

"You were luring me on."

"I was not!"

He pushed himself away from the wall and stood in front of her. "What's your price, Miranda?"

"What's your offer?"

"Not marriage. Pleasure. As much as we both can stand."

"No. That kind of pleasure is temporary. And, when it's over, painful."

"Admit it, Miranda." He put his hands on her shoulders and gave her a shake. "You don't want me, you want something from me."

Why had she told him she wanted him? She should have lied about that, if only for self-protection. The other lies had come easily enough, once he'd made her mad.

How dare he talk about Maude that way! And how dare he think she was after his money! "No, that's not true! I don't want anything that belongs to you." She spun on her heel, but she didn't get far before Stuart's arms encircled her waist again.

She shouldn't have turned her back on him. The sneaky villain was dropping small kisses on her shoulder. Miranda stiffened her back and shrugged. "Don't do that. It tickles."

Stuart stopped nuzzling and pulled her against him, resting his chin on the top of her head. "Where are you going?"

"To my room." She'd learned all she could handle about Stuart for one night.

"It's too early for you to go home. It's not even ten o'clock yet." He pushed her hair behind her ear and began nibbling on her earlobe. "Stay with me tonight, Miranda," he whispered.

She arched her back and turned her head into his shoulder to stop him from breathing in her ear. It worked, for a second or two. She'd almost caught her breath when Stuart began using his magical mouth on the sensitive curve of her neck. Miranda's knees suddenly had the consistency of toasted marshmallows.

Before they buckled, he grasped her waist and turned her around. "Stay," he repeated, his voice husky.

"N-no, I can't." Her breathless response sounded anything but firm, even to her ears. She tried again. In a stronger voice she said, "I'm not interested in a vacation fling."

He kissed her on the nose. "But you want me."

"Wh-what makes you think that?" He couldn't tell that his touch was making her heartbeat erratic, could he?

"You told me so, remember?" He pulled her against him, so that her cheek was resting on the cool white linen of his tuxedo shirt.

Miranda tried to tear herself away, but he tightened his hold, pinning her arms within the circle of his. She abandoned her weak attempt to escape him as the warmth of his body spread into hers. She sniffed delicately, taking in the musky masculine scent of him.

He stood with legs slightly parted so that she was caught within the hard prison of his thighs, her soft body intimately molded against the length of his. Whether from Maude's training or from some inherited womanly artifice, her body eagerly responded to each cue offered by his.

She gave a tremulous sigh and closed her eyes. Stuart moved his large hands to cup her bottom, freeing Miranda's arms. One hand trembled on his chest, while the other stroked the line of his jaw, then traced the outline of his mouth. She heard him groan deep in his throat and felt his lips close on her fingers. He sucked gently, drawing the tips into his mouth. He nibbled lightly on her fingertips while his hands moved up and down her naked back.

The exquisite sensations coursing through each and every one of her nerve endings were almost painful. Miranda sought relief from the sensuous assault by withdrawing her hand and opening her eyes. When she looked up at him sne saw his dark eyes were half-closed and his breathing was shallow. A dull red flush was visible beneath the faint stubble of his beard.

She felt a rush of feminine power when she realized he wanted her, too. And he wanted her for herself, not for anything her parents could do for him.

His arms tightened around her, and she quivered in anticipation of his kiss. Stuart's mouth touched her lips softly, then more insistently, until her lips parted in mute surrender. He thrust his tongue into her mouth again and again. Miranda thought she might die from the pleasure of it.

When Stuart finally released her mouth, she used her freedom to press kisses on each of his eyelids in turn. He busied his lips with the pulse point frantically beating on her vulnerable neck. Miranda knew that if this was real life, she'd have to stop soon. But it was only a play, make-believe. The fire smoldering between them wasn't real—she couldn't get burned.

Greedily, she kissed Stuart again and again, until they both were breathless and gasping for air.

She didn't hear the door open.

"Oops. Sorry. Polly told me I shouldn't come home yet, but I just couldn't stay awake a minute longer."

Miranda jerked herself out of Stuart's arms. He stood there, as calm as if his mother had interrupted a discussion of the stock market.

"Hello, Mother."

Miranda stared at him wide-eyed, her cheeks hot, her lips swollen from his kisses. She couldn't match his composure, not when her pulse was still racing and she'd forgotten how to breathe. Fainting might be a good thing to do, she thought. She swayed.

Stuart grabbed her by the arm as she sagged against his side. "I'd like you to meet Miranda St. James. Miranda, this is Victoria Winslow, my mother."

The sophisticated woman standing in the doorway smiled knowingly. "How do you do? Never mind. You don't have to answer that. I'll just toddle off to bed. Stuart, I'd like to see you in the morning." She walked past them and headed down the hall Miranda assumed led to the bedrooms.

"Sorry, Mother. I'm leaving for Runaway Bay first thing tomorrow morning."

Dazed, Miranda gaped at him. Why hadn't he told her he was leaving San Sebastian? And how could he look and sound so . . . so composed?

"If I'd known that, I would have stayed there," said his mother. Victoria Winslow sounded as cultured as she looked. Miranda took a deep breath and made herself think of snowballs and icicles. The Winslows were a cool pair, but she could be every bit as frosty as they were. Think Grace Kelly, she told herself.

"If you'd called before you came, I would have told you," said Stuart.

His mother sighed. "I'll go back with you."

"No. Miranda's going with me." Stuart pulled her tight against his side, and Miranda's winter scene melted faster than ice cream in hell. "There isn't room on the helicopter for both of you."

Miranda cleared her throat and said, "If your mother wants to go with you, I don't have to go to Jamaica—"

"Yes, you do." He leaned his head down and whispered in her ear, "If you want me to believe all the things you've told me, you do."

Miranda kept quiet. She didn't want to argue with him in front of his mother. But she wasn't going away with him—not with the man whose kisses made her forget he wasn't interested in marriage.

Victoria shifted her gaze to Miranda. "It's all right, Miss St. James. I can see my son when you return. I don't mind spending a few days on San Sebastian. I've been to this resort only once before, a brief trip, for a shareholders' meeting. There are things here I've never seen."

Miranda tensed. "Sugar House?" she asked, glimpsing a new route to her goal.

"Oh, I've seen that. I made a special point to see Sugar House. Have you been there?"

Stuart let go of Miranda so suddenly she almost fell down. She regained her balance and said, "No. I've only read about it."

"Miranda does a lot of reading," Stuart said.

His tone sounded sarcastic to Miranda.

"Do you?" Victoria gave Miranda a puzzled smile. "Would you like to see Sugar House?"

"I'd love to," sighed Miranda. Thank goodness! She'd finally done it—she'd gotten an invitation to Sugar House. One more day and she could tell Stuart everything.

"I wouldn't mind seeing it again, myself," said Victoria. "When you return from Runaway Bay—"

"No," Stuart interrupted.

"Why not?" asked his mother.

"Sugar House isn't open to the public."

"I'm not the public, Stuart, I'm your mother. As well as one of the owners. I'll show Sugar House to Miranda."

Miranda smiled gratefully at Victoria. Stuart wouldn't refuse his mother. During the tour of Sugar House, she'd pop into Maude's bedroom, get the jewels and—

"You forget, Mother. Sugar House belongs to me, not to Island International. And if Miranda wants to see a great house, I'll take her to see Rose Hall while we're in Jamaica."

"You're being rude, Stuart. I wonder why."

Stuart's eyes flashed silver. "Mother—"

"I'm well aware of the fact that Robert left you the house and its contents. I meant I was one of the owners of the resort. It's an owner's duty to keep the guests happy. Miranda's not happy.''

"She's happy.'' He pulled Miranda against his side.

"She's not. She wants to see Sugar House. Don't you, dear?''

"Oh, yes. I'd love to see Sugar House,'' she gushed.

"Of course you would. Probably a lot of people would be interested in seeing where Maude Merrick lived. You really should have tours, Stuart.''

"That's what I thought,'' said Miranda.

Victoria smiled at her. "Great minds...'' She looked at her son. "Stuart?''

His jaw tightened. Miranda was sure she heard his teeth grinding. "All right, Mother. We'll take a quick look around tomorrow morning.''

Victoria arched an eyebrow. "Fine. Now, you two carry on. I'm going to bed.''

"Good night, Mrs. Winslow.''

"Victoria, my dear. Call me Victoria.''

"Good night, Victoria.''

As soon as Victoria disappeared down the hall to her bedroom, Miranda turned to Stuart. "Why did you tell your mother I'm going to Jamaica with you?''

"Because you are.''

"I am not. I told you, I'm not interested in a vacation fling.''

"But you are interested in me, aren't you? You aren't lying about that, are you, Miranda?''

"Uh...no, of course not.''

"Then you want to spend time with me, don't you?''

"Y-yes.'' She'd have to go. She'd trapped herself, and there was no way out that wouldn't make Stuart suspicious. "Oh, all right,'' she said ungraciously. "I'll go with you.''

"I thought you would. We'll leave tomorrow around nine o'clock. Pack your red bikini and a dinner dress."

"How long will we be gone?"

"A day or two. Longer if you decide to deliver on the promises you've made."

"I never promised you anything!"

"No? Just teasing, Miranda?"

"I am not a tease. And if I ever promise you anything, you'll get it." She poked him in the chest with her finger. "I always keep my promises."

Stuart grabbed her hand and held it against his shoulder. "A paragon of virtue, just like Maude Merrick."

Miranda tried to pull her hand away. She was much too susceptible to Stuart's touch. "Why do you keep bringing her up?"

"I'm reminding myself not to make the same mistake my father made."

"I'm going—before I make any more mistakes." When he raised an inquiring eyebrow, she added, "Like agreeing to go to Jamaica with you."

He grinned wickedly. "I'll take you to your suite."

When he returned to the penthouse, Stuart picked up the telephone and dialed Polly's suite. "Polly? Sorry to call so late, but I need you to order the exterminator crew to Sugar House first thing in the morning."

"Oh, dear! Termites?"

"No—Mother. She insisted that I take her and Miranda on a tour."

"I see. But you won't be able to do that if the house is being sprayed with toxic chemicals. I'll take care of it."

"Thanks, Polly."

Stuart was smiling when he hung up. He'd been off-balance earlier, no doubt about it, but he was back in control again now.

Miranda had agreed to go away with him.

## Chapter Six

The next morning, Miranda followed the maître d' to Victoria Winslow's table. She'd been surprised and flattered when Victoria had called earlier to invite her to breakfast. Maybe she hadn't made as big a fool of herself last night as she'd thought.

Besides, Miranda admitted, stepping past a waiter, she couldn't resist learning more about the woman who—along with Maude—had contributed to Stuart's cynical view of women.

Personally, Miranda couldn't imagine what Victoria had done to deserve her son's antagonism. Nor could she understand why Robert Winslow had ever let her go. Miranda had the natural blonde's envy of a gorgeous brunette, and Victoria's black hair and violet eyes would make anyone jealous.

Stuart had told her his father had a weakness for beautiful, sexy women. After seeing Victoria Winslow, Miranda had to agree. Any man who'd married both

Victoria and Maude had to be a connoisseur of feminine charms.

Evidently, Stuart didn't share his father's taste in women. What was it about Robert's two wives that got Stuart's back up? He couldn't really believe that both Victoria and Maude were gold diggers, could he?

The maître d' pulled out a chair and seated Miranda. Victoria, dressed in a linen trouser suit, appeared chic and poised. She really was a classy lady, thought Miranda, hoping she looked half as elegant in her own silk slacks and sweater.

Victoria smiled. "I'm so glad you could join me, Miranda." She waited until the waiter gave Miranda a menu, then continued, "Are you looking forward to your trip to Jamaica?"

"Yes, I am." Miranda gave the menu a quick look. "I'll have a croissant, orange juice and coffee, please," she told the waiter. Victoria ordered wheat toast and black coffee.

After the waiter left, Miranda added, "I hope it's not interfering with your visit with Stuart, though."

"Don't worry about it. Stuart has never been a dutiful son—not to me, anyway. Whatever filial loyalty he felt, he gave to Robert." She laughed ruefully. "Don't look so dismayed. I didn't ask you to breakfast so that I could embarrass you with tales of family discord. It's certainly not your fault that Stuart and I have never been close."

"Why haven't you?" Miranda blurted before she could squelch her curiosity. Chagrined, she continued hastily, "I'm sorry. It's none of my business."

"But it may be, if you and Stuart are as...fond of one another as it seems."

Miranda blushed. "We're not. We only met a few days ago. Stuart and I are barely to the friendship stage."

Victoria raised an eyebrow. "Really? I've never found him passionately embracing a . . . friend in the penthouse foyer before."

Miranda's face grew hotter. She sipped from the icy glass of orange juice the waiter had placed before her and tried to compose her thoughts.

Victoria patted her on the hand. "Forgive me. I couldn't resist teasing you a bit, I'm afraid. You seem like a very nice girl, just the sort I'd like for a daughter-in-law."

"Daughter-in-law?" Miranda almost choked on her orange juice.

"Too soon to talk about such things?"

Too soon to even think about such things, Miranda thought, a little desperately. "Stuart hasn't . . . That is to say, he's not . . . I'm not in love with him." Her stomach knotted. It had to be from embarrassment—she wasn't lying to Victoria.

"No? Too bad. You make such an attractive couple. And you have so much in common."

"We do?"

Victoria nodded as she took a bite of toast. "Polly told me about your interest in movies. Stuart has always been fascinated by motion pictures. He might have gotten involved in the business of moviemaking if he hadn't felt compelled to follow in his father's footsteps. More's the pity."

Miranda shot a questioning look at Victoria. "Why do you say that?"

"Sour grapes, my dear. I was always jealous of Stuart's relationship with his father—and of his father's relationship with Island International."

"Why?"

"I met Robert Winslow when he bought my family's inn on Martha's Vineyard. I always felt like Robert thought of me as part of the deal, and not the most important part, at that."

"You can't mean Stuart's father *bought* you?" Miranda's eyes widened in shock.

Victoria shrugged. "You might say that—although I didn't realize I'd sold myself, at least not right away. It took me years to figure out that when Robert said I was an asset he meant in the balance sheet sense. Robert always paid more attention to the business than he did to me. He was the quintessential workaholic. I'm afraid Stuart is too much like his father at times."

Victoria paused and took a sip of coffee. She gave Miranda a speculative look. "Polly tells me he's been playing more and working less since he met you."

Miranda buttered her croissant and tried to look nonchalant. "Is that right?" She took a bite of the flaky pastry and chewed vigorously. She had to do something to keep a giddy grin off her face.

"I understand he ordered playground equipment, too. Because you pointed out that there was nothing for children to do at San Sebastian."

Miranda swallowed past the lump that had suddenly formed in her throat. "He did?"

Victoria nodded. "You've had a positive influence on my son during your short . . . friendship. Maybe you'll succeed where I failed."

"But you didn't fail—"

"That's sweet of you, but when I was young I spent all my time and energy on my husband—to the neglect of my son, I'm sorry to say. By the time I realized what I'd done, it was too late for me and Stuart."

"It's never too late," Miranda said, just as Stuart arrived at the table.

"Never too late for what?" he asked.

"For you to accept Monarch's latest offer," Victoria said quickly. "I had a thought. They might offer even more for Island International if we said we'd throw in Maude Merrick's island home."

Miranda watched the warmth drain from Stuart's eyes as he stared at his mother. "I'm not selling Island International to Monarch—with or without Sugar House."

Victoria shook her head. "Just like your father."

He ignored her and pulled out Miranda's chair. "Come on, Miranda," he said, helping her to rise. "Let's go to Jamaica."

Miranda's brows knitted in a confused frown. "I thought we were going to tour Sugar House first."

"Not this morning. It turns out the exterminators were scheduled for today. We'll have to put off the tour until another time."

Sighing in apparent resignation, Victoria asked, "When are you coming back?"

"Tomorrow or the day after," Stuart told her.

"We won't miss Classics Night, will we?" asked Miranda, anxiously. She couldn't handle more than a day or two alone with Stuart.

"No, Miranda, you won't miss a thing," Stuart responded dryly.

"Classics Night? Something new?" asked Victoria.

"Yes. Miranda suggested that I show some of my old films at the resort theater periodically."

"What a good idea! Which movie are you going to show? *Casablanca? The Treasure of the Sierra Madre?*"

"No. I decided you were right, Mother. We should exploit San Sebastian's show business connections. So I chose *Forbidden Love* for the first Classics Night."

"*Forbidden Love?*" Miranda squeaked, grabbing the back of the chair for support as her knees threatened to buckle.

Victoria frowned. "I don't remember that title. One of you film buffs will have to enlighten me."

"*Forbidden Love* was Maude Merrick's first and only film, Mother. And the male star—what's his name, Miranda?"

"Tynan Rafferty," whispered Miranda, struggling to appear outwardly composed. She couldn't quell her inner panic. *Forbidden Love* was a melodrama of lovers cruelly separated, then triumphantly reunited in the ultimate Hollywood happy ending.

But it was much more than a mediocre formula film to Miranda. All through her adolescence, she'd watched the movie whenever she was with one parent and lonesome for the other. Everything she cared passionately about was in that film—her parents, her longing for a family, her hopes for a lasting love of her own. She couldn't watch that film here, not with Stuart.

"Tynan Rafferty," he repeated, interrupting her frantic thoughts. "He was Maude's first husband, Mother. He's currently starring in some television series."

"Now that I am familiar with," said Victoria. "*The Adventurers.* Saturday night at nine. I seldom miss it. Oh, my, that certainly says a lot about my social life, doesn't it? Of course, if I had a bigger income, I could find other ways to spend my weekends besides watching television."

Stuart scowled at his mother. "Try needlework, why don't you?"

"Too solitary. I like being with people. Attractive, charming people. Like your—" she winked slyly at Miranda "—friend here."

Miranda gaped at her. *Forbidden Love* and Victoria's blatant matchmaking were conjuring up visions of rose-covered cottages and picket fences. She hadn't come to San Sebastian looking for a husband. Even if she had, Stuart had made it clear he wasn't the marrying kind.

"I like being with Miranda, too," said Stuart, taking Miranda by the arm. "I'll like it even more when we're alone together at Runaway Bay," he whispered in her ear.

Miranda shivered as she felt his hand move to the small of her back and propel her away from his mother. "Now, if you'll excuse us, the helicopter's waiting."

The helicopter ride passed in a blur. All Miranda could think about was that she was alone with Stuart. On San Sebastian, her seduction of him had been part of Maude's fantasy. On Jamaica, his seduction of her might become all too real, if she didn't come up with a plan—fast.

As they entered the lobby of the Runaway Bay resort, Miranda still hadn't decided what to do. She wandered aimlessly around the lobby while Stuart checked them in. She had a sinking feeling he wasn't asking for separate rooms.

Miranda stopped her nervous pacing, her eye caught by the colorful brochures displayed in a stand next to the concierge's desk. She began taking them out one by one. They advertised tours of Rose Hall, day trips to Montego Bay, Kingston, the Blue Mountains. Glass-bottomed boat trips competed for attention with snorkeling and scuba-diving lessons. The germ of an idea began to sprout in her brain.

An hour later Miranda closed her eyes and let the beauty salon attendants have their way with her. She'd headed straight for the salon the minute Stuart had left her alone. She needed coddling.

She'd been somewhat relieved to find out Stuart really did have business to take care of at the resort, but it was too much to hope that the business would last all day and all night.

Miranda was still clutching the tour brochures as the salon attendant went over the services available. She asked for the works, and they started her off with a trip to the sauna. Wrapped in a towel, she lay on a wooden shelf and waited for the dry heat to drain away the tension knotting her muscles.

Dinner with Stuart and breakfast with his mother had left her wound up like a top. Sometime during those two encounters, she'd completely lost control.

A dinner invitation to Sugar House, a quick trip to Maude's old bedroom to recover the jewels from the hidden safe—it had all seemed so simple five days ago.

Nothing had gone right since she set foot on San Sebastian. Stuart had resisted her best imitations of silver screen sirens. He didn't live at Sugar House, and fate had conspired with bug sprayers to keep her and everyone else away from it.

She sighed. She was no closer to recovering Maude's jewels than the day she'd arrived on Stuart's island.

No closer? Try farther away than ever. Now she wasn't even on the right island. And she was definitely in the wrong movie. She'd envisioned a caper plot, like *Topkapi* or *To Catch a Thief*. Not *Pillow Talk*.

She sat up and leaned her back against the wooden slats. Maude's jewels weren't the real problem, she forced herself to admit. Stuart was. Not Stuart, exactly, but the way he was making her feel—reckless and lighthearted, eager and apprehensive.

Why had she ever agreed to come away with him? She should have stayed on San Sebastian and tried her hand at breaking and entering. That wouldn't have been nearly as dangerous as being at Runaway Bay with Stuart.

If she ever ended up in his bedroom, if they made love, she'd fall in love with him, and it wouldn't be an act.

She couldn't fall in love with Stuart. He'd made it clear he didn't want marriage. And Miranda didn't want an affair. She had been raised by Maude Merrick, after all, and Maude had old-fashioned ideas about love and marriage. Ideas Stuart did not share, although she was almost sure he didn't know very much about love. He seemed to think it was something men bought.

Did all men feel like that? Had Tynan? Was that why he needed to be rich, richer than Maude? Maybe that was why Maude had looked for security in a man's wealth. Lack of it had driven away the first man she ever loved.

Miranda wished she'd paid more attention to Maude's discourses on the male ego. Her mother had very definite opinions—gleaned from hands-on experience—about what made men attractive. And she had to admit Maude had always placed a man's ability to support her close to the top of the list.

Stuart appeared to be rich enough. Miranda smiled. Considering the fact that she was currently unemployed, he'd have to be destitute to fail that test.

Regardless of what Stuart thought, a man's money wasn't Maude's only criteria. Love was factored into the equation, too. Maude really had loved all her husbands. Love wasn't enough, though. There had to be something more—commitment, trust. Tynan had loved Maude, but he'd still let his ego get in the way of happy ever after.

If she was right, and Stuart didn't know how to love, was she the one to teach him? She'd just reminded herself that love had to be grounded on trust. She'd lied to him. He hated liars. He'd never trust her.

The door to the sauna opened, and an attendant said in the lilting Jamaican accent, "Come with me, miss."

Miranda followed the woman to a small room and climbed onto the massage table. The masseuse rubbed strawberry-scented oil onto her heated skin and began to work on her still-tense muscles.

Who wouldn't be tense? She was only hours, maybe only minutes, away from being alone with Stuart again. Surely he'd want to continue where they'd been interrupted last night. She wasn't at all certain she'd be able to resist him. And she had to resist—or risk losing much more than Maude's jewels.

Miranda swallowed a moan as the masseuse pummeled her back. Heat seeped into her, leaving her body limp—and not because of the sauna. Not entirely, anyway. Every time she thought of Stuart and his kisses, she got hotter.

If only she knew what he wanted.

Her. He wanted her. She couldn't keep her lips from curving into a smug smile. At least that part of the plan had worked. She should be satisfied with her small victory—she'd made a very attractive man, a man who had no ulterior motive, want her.

But for how long?

Miranda winced as her shoulder muscles were ruthlessly pounded. She was very much afraid she wanted forever. Did he?

She closed her eyes and tried to make her mind a blank. If only she could be like Scarlett O'Hara and think about that tomorrow! But she couldn't, not with a long tropical night stretching between now and then. She had to think of a way to avoid paying the price for being a successful femme fatale.

Stuart found her shortly after she'd had her hair washed with coconut milk shampoo. She was wrapped in herbal scented towels, her face smeared with peach moisturizer, having her nails manicured.

"You smell like a fruit salad," he said, dropping a key into her lap. "That's to the owner's suite." He leaned down and dropped a quick kiss on her mouth. "But you taste like a woman," he whispered, his breath teasing her earlobe.

"Are you finished with your business?" she asked, a little bewildered. How could he want to kiss her when she was covered with goop?

"Not quite. I should be done in a couple of hours. How about you? How much longer will this stuff take?"

"Another hour or so," she told him. "I have our day all planned." She nodded toward the brochures on the vanity table.

"Have you? What are we going to do?"

"We'll grab a quick lunch here, then go to see Rose Hall. After that we'll take a glass-bottom boat to the coral reef, then drive to Montego Bay for dinner and dancing. Tomorrow, I thought we could have an early morning snorkeling lesson, then take a picnic lunch to Dunn's River Falls. We'll come back here for the weekly beach party—complete with steel band and limbo dancing." She paused for breath. "What do you think?"

"I think we're going to be very busy." He laughed, nodded to the manicurist and walked away.

Miranda frowned at Stuart's receding back as he walked away. What was so funny?

* * *

Stuart stared through the windshield of the Rolls and tried to concentrate on staying on the left side of the road. Every time his thoughts strayed from driving, the car drifted to the right. A traffic accident was all he needed to complete a very strange day.

The business that had brought him to Runaway Bay had been bad enough. But he'd demonstrated a definite tendency toward masochism when he'd asked Miranda to come with him. He never should have brought her to Jamaica. He'd have been better off leaving her on San Sebastian and trusting Polly and security to keep her out of Sugar House.

Stuart grinned. One thing was sure—after the frenetic pace she'd set for them, it was obvious she had no intention of ending up in the same hotel room with him, at least not until he was too exhausted to take advantage of the situation. It had taken him awhile to figure out why that pleased him. Then he'd realized it showed her lack of experience. If Miranda was a real adventuress, one more seduction wouldn't be a big deal.

Instead of using sex to get what she wanted, she was trying very hard to keep him out of her bed. She'd even tried to get him drunk. He shook his head in amazement. He'd stopped that little ploy by reminding her he was driving.

The little minx might have hoisted herself on her own petard, he thought, his grin widening to a smile. She'd had several fancy rum drinks over the course of the evening. By the time the last nightclub had shooed them out, she'd begun to enunciate very carefully. And she'd been a little wobbly on the dance floor—he'd had to hold her very close when they'd danced the last dance.

He stifled a groan, remembering how she'd felt in his arms. Bringing her with him had definitely been a mistake. The more time he spent with her the harder it was to remember what he'd learned from his father's mistakes—real women are trouble. He glanced at Miranda, snuggled against his side, her head on his shoulder. Especially this one—she'd even replaced Ava Gardner and Marilyn Monroe in his dreams.

Hell, she'd charmed everyone she'd met—Polly, Tommy, his mother. Why should he be immune?

"I had a wonderful time," she said, her words slightly slurred.

Stuart's lips twitched. He'd had a great time, too. Even if her transparent attempts to keep him at a distance had been a little hard on the ego at first. Then he'd realized she wouldn't be working so hard at it if she was truly indifferent to him.

"The story of the White Witch of Rose Hall was fascinating," she sighed.

"Uh-huh."

"You're a very good dancer."

"Mm."

Stuart turned the car into the Runaway Bay resort. He pulled up to the main entrance and stopped. "Miranda, honey, sit up. We're home."

Miranda jerked upright. She focused her eyes and watched in alarm as Stuart got out of the car and bounded around to open her door. "Payday," she muttered.

Stuart couldn't spend all his time behind his desk; he had too much energy left. She, on the other hand, was definitely out of shape. She was so tired she was cross-eyed. At least she'd managed to stay sober. After her first drink she had whispered to the bartender to leave the rum out of her piña coladas.

The car door opened and Stuart reached in to help her out. She smiled weakly as he took her by the arm and marched her up the stairs and into the lobby. He was heading for the private elevator to the owner's suite with unseemly haste, she thought indignantly.

Miranda tugged frantically on his sleeve. "Wait. Don't you want a nightcap?"

He stopped and looked at her, a bemused expression on his face. At least she thought it was bemused—but she wasn't focusing all that well. "Not particularly," he said.

"Well, I do," she said, her tone belligerent. She carefully removed her arm from under his and started toward the lobby bar.

"Miranda, sweetheart, I think you've had enough."

"No, I haven't," she said and kept walking. Why was he calling her names? Honey. Sweetheart. Her lip curled. If he thought that was all it took to get her into his bed—

"Watch out!" Stuart grabbed her just before she bumped into the doorjamb. He steered her through the swinging doors and sat her down at a table.

"I'll have a piña colada," she told the waiter.

"Brandy," said Stuart. Then he didn't say anything. He just looked at her, his gray eyes shooting silver sparks in the candlelight. When the drinks came, he raised his glass in a silent salute, but he still didn't open his mouth.

His mouth distracted her for a moment. One thing she had to give him, he was a darn good kisser. Her poignant sigh turned into a noisy, openmouthed yawn. She belatedly covered her mouth with her hand. "Sorry," she mumbled.

Stuart grinned at her. He looked just like the Cheshire cat. Miranda frowned. Or was it the cat who ate the canary? Smart, sassy, sure of himself. That's how he looked. She shook her head to clear away the cobwebs spinning there.

"Well?" She tapped the table with her scarlet fingernails. "Did you take care of your business this morning?"

"More or less." His brows came together in that sexy scowl she'd come to know and—

Miranda censored that thought and concentrated on Stuart's troubled look. "What's wrong, Stuart?"

He tangled his fingers with hers. "You don't want to hear about my problems."

"Yes, I do." Keep talking, sweet talker. Miranda swallowed a giggle and concentrated on appearing sympathetic. "Sometimes it helps to talk about things," she coaxed.

He took a deep breath. "Okay, you asked for it. The assistant manager at this resort resigned."

"Can't he be replaced?"

"Sure. That's not the problem. Why he quit is the problem. Monarch Hotels. Shortly after my father died last year, they offered to buy us out. Mother was all for it."

"You weren't."

"No. Monarch made a fair enough offer for the stock, but I know how they operate. They would have fired at least a third of Island International's employees. A multinational conglomerate wouldn't care that the resorts are the biggest employer on some of the islands, the only employer on others, like San Sebastian."

Stuart cupped the brandy snifter in his hand and swirled the amber liquid. He continued, "For our employees, getting laid off means more than losing a job, it means losing homes and friends—maybe even families. I couldn't let that happen."

As she listened to Stuart, Miranda was picturing scenes from a Caribbean version of *The Grapes of Wrath*. She blinked back tears. "Oh, Stuart. Of course you couldn't."

"No. So I turned down the offer, once I got control of a majority of the stock."

Stock. Hadn't Maude owned some stock? Miranda frowned, unable to remember. "I don't understand." She used her cocktail napkin to brush the moisture from her eyelashes. "If you turned down the offer months ago, why did the assistant manager resign this week?"

"Monarch hasn't given up. They know Mother wants to sell, and they've continued negotiations with her. As long as the possibility exists that she'll sell her forty percent, or that she'll convince me to sell, the rumors keep flying, and the people who work for me are uncertain about their futures. It's bad for business and lousy for employee morale."

"Have you explained all this to Victoria? Surely if she knew, she'd do something to stop the takeover rumors."

"She understands the situation. She doesn't care."

"I don't believe that. She seemed like a very caring person to me."

Stuart snorted. "You heard her. She wants money. More than she's getting from Island International stock dividends."

"Maybe she just wants attention. If Monarch is courting her..."

"I'm not taking that guilt trip, Miranda. Maybe I haven't spent much time with her lately, but if she's lonely, it's her own fault. She could cultivate outside interests—other than jet-setting with the ultra rich."

"She said she's a people person. Maybe she should get a job. You said she used to work with your father at the resorts."

"That was a long time ago."

"Maybe you should encourage her to work again."

"Too late. She's convinced a woman should be supported by a man—father, husband or son." He turned Miranda's hand up and stroked her palm with his thumb. "What about you? Do you expect some man to support you?" he asked.

"No. I can take care of myself." She tugged, but he held onto her hand.

"I guess you can, at that," he agreed smoothly. "Two weeks at an Island International resort don't come cheap. But aren't you unemployed now?"

She shrugged. "I'm between jobs. I'll get another."

Stuart lifted his glass to his lips and sipped the brandy. "How did you get the job with Wisdom's estate?"

Miranda frowned. Had she mentioned that she'd worked for Waldo Wisdom's estate? She must have. "Ty—someone recommended me."

"Someone? Who?"

"One of my professors at UCLA. But I probably would have gotten the job without any recommendation, once Daniel realized—" She bit her tongue.

"Daniel?" Stuart's eyes narrowed.

Miranda cleared her throat and tried to pay attention to what she was saying. "Daniel Eberhart. He was the attorney for the estate. He hired me."

"Why did he want you to get the job?"

"He . . . had his reasons." She lowered her eyes.

"He wanted you."

Stuart sounded angry. "He *pretended* he wanted me."

"Why?"

"I don't want to talk about Daniel." She didn't want to talk about anything anymore. She was having too much trouble keeping up with the changing moods—hers and his.

"Were you involved?" he asked.

She shook her head, then wished she hadn't. It made her dizzy. "Not for long."

"What happened? Wasn't he a successful lawyer?"

"Not as successful as he wanted to be." She gazed at him. He wasn't jealous, was he? "Why are you so interested in Daniel? I wasn't."

"You weren't what?"

"Interested. In Daniel," she enunciated. Her bottom lip quivered. "He didn't love me."

"Love is important to you?"

"Yes."

"More important than money?"

"Of course," she said haughtily. "I'd never marry someone I didn't love."

He sneered. "Or somebody who couldn't support you." He ignored her outraged gasp and continued. "You won't continue your career after you're married, will you?"

"I certainly will." Now there was no doubt about it—he was definitely turning nasty. "At least until I have children."

"You paint a pretty picture, Miranda." His gaze raked over her. "But I'm not buying it."

"Who asked you to?" Her voice shook. He grinned at her—nastily. "And it's not for sale, anyway! Your mother was right! You are like your father!"

He clamped his hand on her wrist. "What's that supposed to mean?"

"You both think love's for sale."

"Isn't it?"

"Not mine!"

He leaned forward and took her chin in his hand. "Tell me this, Miranda. If you're such an old-fashioned girl, why did you agree to come away with me?"

"Because I...because you and I..." She glared at him. "If you think I'm such a terrible person, why did you ask me?"

He tossed back the rest of his brandy. "I don't think you're a terrible person. Let's go to bed."

# Chapter Seven

Miranda dumped her drink in Stuart's lap.

She heard the waiter's horrified gasp. It only took one look at Stuart's face to convince her that retreat would be the better part of valor.

Heart pounding, she rose quickly and headed for the exit. As she pushed through the swinging doors on her way out of the lounge, she risked a glance over her shoulder and discovered Stuart was coming after her, his trademark scowl firmly in place.

Miranda ran to the penthouse elevator and leapt into the waiting car. Stuart arrived just as the doors swished shut.

By the time she reached the owner's suite, the adrenalin surging through her blood had cleared her sleep-fogged brain enough for Miranda to realize she might have made a little mistake. Pouring a piña colada into a man's lap was probably not the best way to cool his passion.

Not that Stuart had been all that passionate. He'd been more insulting than ardent. So what had he expected?

Not wet pants.

She covered her face with her hands and moaned. *Sticky* wet pants.

At the sound of a key turning in the lock, Miranda whirled around. Stuart stood in the doorway, his tuxedo trousers in his hand, his muscular thighs exposed to her gaze.

"Why?" he asked through gritted teeth, waving his trousers in front of him. "I just want to know why, Miranda."

She jerked her eyes to his face.

"I'm waiting, Miranda." He didn't look as if he'd wait for long.

Miranda drew herself up regally. "Please leave my room." She giggled, spoiling her try at dignity.

"Your room? This is the owner's suite—and you're not the owner. I am."

"You can't stay here."

"Oh, yes, I can. If you don't like it, get yourself another room." Stuart's eyes followed her as she picked up the telephone on the end table next to the sofa. "Don't waste a call, Miranda. The hotel is completely booked."

He advanced toward her, his dripping pants held out in front of him.

Miranda dropped the receiver onto its cradle and backed away from him. "W-what are you going to do?"

"I'll think of something. I always get even." He leered wickedly.

She stopped her retreat and tilted her chin up defiantly. "Don't touch me!"

"Why not? You like it when I touch you." He threw his pants onto a chair and kept coming. "Don't you?"

She ignored the question. "Stuart!" Half-dressed, he looked awfully funny. Grinning, she stomped her foot in mock anger. "Put your pants on!"

He stopped long enough to look down at his white shirttail, bare thighs and black socks. When he looked at her again, his lips were twitching. "I'd rather take yours off," he said, wiggling his eyebrows like Groucho Marx.

Miranda scurried behind a sofa. "That's not funny."

"It's not? Well, you said I never learned how to play." He came to a stop in front of the sofa. "Why don't you teach me how, Miranda?"

He held out his hand. She shook her head and put both her hands behind her back. "Not until you apologize."

His eyes widened. "Apologize? Me?"

"Yes."

"For what? I didn't pour rum and coconut milk in your lap."

"No, but you did call me a gold digger."

"No, I didn't."

"Yes, you did."

He shook his head. "Maybe your guilty conscience affects your hearing."

"I don't have a guilty conscience. I haven't done anything wr—"

Stuart hurdled over the back of the sofa and grabbed for her. His sudden move sent them both to the floor in a tangle of arms and legs. After a brief tussle, Stuart ended up flat on his back, with her draped across his body. She flattened her palms against his chest and tried to lever herself off of him.

He wrapped his arms around her and growled in her ear, "Where do you think you're going?"

"I'm not going to bed with you," she said weakly. Having Stuart supine beneath her was doing funny things to her pulse rate.

"Who asked?"

"You did. In the bar."

"I said let's go to bed—I didn't say together. This suite has two bedrooms, Miranda."

"I knew that." The fight went out of her, and she buried her head against his chest. Keeping her wrapped in his arms, Stuart managed to stand up. He molded her tightly against him, making her aware of a definite dampness in his nether regions.

"What's the matter?" he asked.

"Nothing. I guess I'm just tired."

"Tired or scared?"

She looked at him. "Scared? Of what?"

"Me. You've been running away from me all day." He loosened his hold but kept her in the circle of his arms. "Did you change your mind?"

"About what?"

"Wanting me."

Miranda jerked out of his arms. "I never should have told you that." Suddenly the room began to spin. She clutched at Stuart and moaned, "I don't feel well."

"I'm not surprised," he said, stroking her back. "You had too much to drink."

She rested her head on his shoulder. "No, I didn't." He hadn't realized she'd only drunk one real drink. But even without the rum, the sweet drinks she'd had were making her queasy.

His eyes narrowed. "Oh, then you're sober."

"Of course I'm sober. I never get drunk." She closed her eyes, but opened them quickly when she felt Stuart's tongue tracing the curve of her left earlobe.

"Then I wouldn't be taking unfair advantage if I—"

She leaned away from him. "Yes, you would."

"What did you say?"

"I said, maybe you're right. I may have had one too many."

"Two too many—we'd both be better off if you hadn't ordered that last drink."

She snickered. "You can let me go now."

"In a minute. Maybe." He pulled her against him again. "Stop laughing at me, Miranda."

"I'm sorry I poured a drink in your lap," she said meekly, looking at him.

"Are you?" His silver eyes glinted as he returned her gaze.

"No. Not really. You...you look so cute with your knobby knees hanging out." She collapsed against him, laughing uncontrollably.

After a second, his shoulders started to shake and he joined in. Still chuckling, Stuart picked her up and dropped her onto the sofa. Miranda sank into the cushions, weak from laughter. Stuart vaulted over the back of the sofa and sat next to her, his bare legs stretched out and crossed at the ankles.

He lifted one leg up, bent his knee and brought it close to his face. After a thorough inspection, he straightened his leg and said, "So, you don't like my knobby knees?"

"You have great legs, Stuart," she assured him. "I was only teasing about your knees."

"Great legs, huh?"

She slanted a look at him and caught him smirking.

"Any other of my body parts you'd care to comment on?" he asked innocently.

Her cheeks grew warm. "No."

"Come on, Miranda. We'll make a game of it. You said I needed to learn how to play. I'll start." He reached over and hitched her blue silk skirt up an inch or two. "You have great legs, too," he said, casually resting his hand on her knee.

She pushed his hand away and smoothed her skirt down. "Thank you." She looked at him again. He was waiting expectantly. Miranda's heart twisted. Playing games with Stuart might be playing with fire, but she wanted to be the one to make him laugh.

Miranda swallowed the lump in her throat. One minute she wanted to laugh, the next minute she felt like weeping. She wasn't drunk, she was exhausted. That was what was making her overemotional, not the thought of a grown man who didn't know how to have fun.

She tried to give Stuart an exaggerated once-over, but she couldn't tear her eyes away from his mouth. "You have a sexy mouth," she told him, tracing his warm lips with her finger.

"Do I?" Her eyes almost crossed as he brought his mouth close to hers. "I think yours may be sexy, too. I'm not sure. I need to taste it before I decide."

He kissed her—slowly, thoroughly, molding her lips to his. Miranda's eyelids drifted shut as she savored the taste of him.

"Sexy mouth, all right," he said, his voice a husky whisper.

Miranda opened her eyes slowly and looked into his. She *was* playing with fire—and it was getting hotter every minute.

"Soft, too." He pulled her across his lap. "Your turn."

"I like your noble nose." To prove it, she kissed the tip of it.

He touched where she'd kissed. "Why noble?"

"It's very impressive."

"Are you saying I have a big nose? Never mind. Some of your parts aren't exactly small." He stared lewdly at her chest.

Miranda knew he meant his leer to be funny, but her breasts didn't—they swelled in anticipation of his touch.

"It's my turn, isn't it? I almost forgot." He looked her up and down. "I have to say it, Miranda. You've got a great pair of—"

"Stuart!"

"—shoulders. I do admire your shoulders, darlin'," he drawled.

She crossed her arms over her breasts and looked at him. He might be able to make jokes, but she wasn't the only one experiencing swollen body parts. She squirmed. He groaned. Miranda took pity on him and sat still.

"I like your eyes," she told him. "Especially when they look like molten silver."

His eyebrows shot up. "When do they look like that?" He put a finger on her parted lips. "No, don't tell me. I know—when I look at you. Like this."

His gaze moved slowly over her, making her nerve endings tingle. He stopped when his eyes met hers again. "Your eyes are like the ocean. Always changing—sometimes as blue as a summer day, other times dark and stormy."

"What color are they now?"

"The color of love." Stuart bent his head and captured her mouth again. Miranda's breath caught in her throat and she swallowed convulsively. He was right, she thought dazedly. She did love him.

How had that happened? When had it happened? Miranda sighed and parted her lips. She couldn't think.

With Stuart's warm mouth moving on hers, she didn't want to think, she only wanted to feel.

When Stuart finally ended the kiss, he took a deep breath and asked, "What's the score?"

"Score?" she repeated, dizzy from his kisses and her heart-stopping discovery.

"Who's winning the game?"

"Game?" She bit her lip. He'd played a game for her. If he could learn how to play, he could learn how to love. But could he love her? No, she told herself, she'd lied to him. He hated liars.

"Miranda?"

"You are," she said brokenly. "I don't deserve to win."

"Why do you say that? Are you all right?"

She shook her head. "No. I'm a terrible person."

He laughed softly. "You're not terrible—just a little tipsy, that's all."

She looked at him, her lips trembling. "Yes, I am terrible. You said I was."

He kissed her gently on the forehead. "I lied."

"You never lie. You're a stickler for the truth."

"Who told you that?"

"I don't know. I must have read it somewhere." She took a deep breath and closed her eyes. This time when the room began to spin, she kept her eyes tightly shut and let the darkness overcome her.

"Miranda." Stuart kissed her again. No response. His Sleeping Beauty was out for the count.

Frowning, Stuart looked at Miranda, snuggled trustingly in his arms. She was beautiful, no doubt about it—and she was sleeping. But she wasn't his. And he wasn't anyone's Prince Charming. Heroes didn't steal.

Miranda sighed and turned her face into his chest. She looked so sweet and innocent. Why couldn't she be what she seemed?

He cradled her in his arms and stood up, striding purposefully into one of the bedrooms. As he carefully placed her on the bed, she murmured, "I love..."

His heart pounding, Stuart shook her gently. "What did you say? Who do you love?"

Her only answer was another sigh. Stuart shook his head. He must have heard wrong. She didn't love him. She was here with him for one reason, and one reason only—to get to Sugar House and Maude's jewels. Miranda might be dreaming of love, but he wouldn't be the man in her dreams.

Staring at her lying gracefully on the bed, he couldn't help but wonder what it would be like to be loved by Miranda. He reached out and smoothed a strand of hair away from her face. She turned her head, trapping his hand beneath her cheek. "Not like Daniel," she muttered, her brows knitting into a frown.

Stuart jerked his hand back. Who wasn't like Daniel? Him? How wasn't he like Daniel? Not as lovable? Not as rich?

He wasn't jealous, Stuart told himself. No way. He didn't care how Miranda felt about him. Why should he? She'd lose interest soon enough if she knew he wasn't as wealthy as the luxurious resorts he owned might make it appear. And if that didn't do the trick, if she ever found out he'd stolen her mother's jewelry...

Maybe he should tell her what he'd done and see how she reacted. She might understand. When he'd told her about Monarch, she'd seemed genuinely sympathetic. Maybe she could forgive him if he made it clear he'd taken the jewels to save the business for all the employees, not just for himself. She might even help him convince Maude to let him leave the jewels with the bank for another few months—

Don't be a chump, Winslow, he told himself. He couldn't even think about confessing to Maude Merrick's daughter. He couldn't trust Miranda—she was nothing but a beautiful schemer, just like her mother. Hadn't she tried to seduce him into inviting her to Sugar House? She'd backed down soon enough when the venue had changed to Jamaica. And she hadn't told him who she was, had she?

She might be kind to children and maybe she wasn't as greedy as her mother—yet. But she'd learn quick enough. All she needed was a little more experience and she'd be a full-fledged siren just like Maude, capable of luring any number of men to financial ruin.

Not him, though. He was on to her game. If he told her about the jewels, she'd tell her mother. Maude would surely descend upon the bank demanding their return. Without its collateral, the bank would call in the loan. That's all it would take for Monarch and Victoria to force him to sell out.

Miranda moaned softly and turned onto her stomach, twisting her dress around her. He should get her out of her clothes—she'd be uncomfortable if he didn't. Stuart slipped the sandals off her feet, then reached for the zipper of her dress. He pulled it down a few inches, his knuckles grazing the sinuous curve of her spine. His body tightened in response to the silky warmth of her skin.

Undressing Miranda no longer seemed like such a good idea. The game had been fun while it lasted, but playtime was over. Jerking the zipper up, he turned on his heel and left the room.

* * *

Miranda groaned and pulled a pillow over her face, trying to muffle the strident sound of the telephone. Her head was pounding and someone had stuck her eyelashes together with glue. She felt as if she'd slept in her clothes.

She cautiously slit open one eye and looked down at herself. She *had* slept with her clothes on! Her beautiful blue dress was crumpled and twisted around her.

She sat up slowly and listened. The telephone had stopped ringing. Stuart must have answered it.

Stuart! He'd put her to bed. She looked at her wrinkled dress again—obviously he hadn't taken advantage of her. Why would he? He must have thought she'd drunk too much and passed out. Not the way to attract any man, much less a gentleman like Stuart.

Miranda sat up, swung her legs over the side of the bed and padded to the bathroom. She felt as if she really had drunk too much the night before. Her head was pounding. Surely she'd feel better once she'd taken some aspirin and showered.

She didn't. If anything, she felt worse. She'd had time to think about the things she'd done last night. She'd poured a drink in his lap! She'd played a silly game with him. She'd fallen asleep in her clothes.

She'd fallen in love.

Miranda sighed. Her head ached and her heart was breaking. After the way she'd behaved last night, Stuart wouldn't want to have anything more to do with her. Even if he was willing to overlook her scandalous behavior and spend the day with her, what good would it do? He still didn't know the worst about her. He'd never forgive her for lying to him.

Stuart was standing next to her rumpled bed fully dressed in dark suit and tie when she came out of the bathroom. Miranda pulled the belt of her robe tighter, feeling strangely vulnerable wearing nothing but her yellow silk robe. He did not look as though he was in a forgiving mood.

She eyed his clothes again. Definitely not resort wear. "I guess we're not going to Dunn's River Falls this morning."

"I'm not. I have to go back to San Sebastian immediately. That's what I came to tell you." His voice was flat and his eyes didn't meet hers.

Miranda reached out her hand, but she stopped short of touching him. She didn't want to feel him flinch. "I'm really sorry about last night, Stuart. I know I made a fool of myself. Can't we spend the day as we planned?"

"No, we can't," he said briskly.

"Oh, Stuart, I really am sorry," she murmured sadly.

"You don't need to keep apologizing. I'm not leaving here because of you. There's an emergency at the resort—the hotel's overbooked."

"Oh, I see. Well, it should only take me a few minutes to dress and pack."

"You don't have to go back with me," he said. "Stay here and finish your sight-seeing."

Miranda looked at him, sure her eyes must reflect her misery. "It wouldn't be any fun without you."

"Right," he said, his tone skeptical. He looked at his watch. "It won't be much fun on San Sebastian, either, if we have guests camped out in the lobby. If you stay here we can use your suite to ease the overcrowding."

Miranda stuck out her chin. He might be annoyed with her, but she wasn't about to be left behind. She had business on San Sebastian. "No. I don't want to stay here alone. And that suite is mine—I worked hard for it. Remember Tommy?'' she asked.

He threw up his hands. ''All right, you win. I'll take you back with me, but you'll have to hurry. The helicopter's standing by.''

He turned and walked out of the room. Miranda chewed her bottom lip anxiously. He might have played games with her last night, but he was all business this morning. She said a quick prayer that he meant what he said—that he wasn't leaving Jamaica because of her. Hoping he'd been aloof only because he was preoccupied with the crisis on San Sebastian, Miranda hurriedly dressed and packed.

By the time the helicopter landed, Miranda didn't know what hurt more—her heart or her head. The headache had hung on tenaciously, and Stuart hadn't thawed one iota. He'd been silent and brooding the whole trip.

He jumped from the helicopter the minute it touched down, ducking to avoid the still spinning rotors. He ran to a waiting Jeep, leaving it to the pilot to help Miranda to the ground. She ran after him, not bothering with her luggage. He looked surprised when she jumped into the Jeep next to him, but at least he didn't make her get out. She followed him into the hotel, only a few steps behind. He wasn't going to get away from her—he was the man she loved.

Stuart strode up to the concierge's desk. ''What's going on, Raoul?''

''Everything's under control now, Mr. Winslow.''

''Exactly what was out of control?''

''Computer glitch. That machine overbooked the resort.''

''How bad?''

''We had four more couples than we had rooms.''

"What did you do with them?"

"Ms. Winslow took care of everything."

Stuart looked relieved. "I should have known Polly could handle things."

"Not Miss Polly. Your mother," Raoul informed him. "She moved out of the owner's suite and put guests there—she also put people in Miss Polly's suite, and Miss St. James's suite, too."

"Mother?" At Raoul's nod, Stuart narrowed his eyes. "She moved people into the family suites?"

"Yes, sir. And Miss St. James's rooms," Raoul repeated.

Miranda frowned when she heard that she'd lost her suite anyway. She opened her mouth to protest, but Stuart was still talking to Raoul.

"That only accounts for three couples—I thought you said there were four."

"That's right, there was one honeymoon couple left over. Ms. Winslow put them in the Maude Merrick suite."

"Maude—" Stuart shoved his hand through his hair. "We don't have a Maude Merrick suite."

"We do now. At Sugar House."

"My mother put guests in Sugar House?" Stuart roared.

"Yes, and she moved you and Miss St. James there, too."

Miranda had to bite her cheeks to keep from chortling out loud. Suddenly, she felt much better. She'd reached her goal after all—without resorting to breaking the law. She was a guest at Sugar House. She'd have the jewels before the day was out and then she could tell Stuart everything—including that she loved him.

"Where is Mother?" A muscle twitched in Stuart's jaw.

"Sugar House. She's acting as concierge for that part of the resort. Polly is there, too, helping her."

"Wait here, Miranda. I've got to talk to Mother."

"I'm going with you." Miranda gave him a fierce look, daring him to object. "Raoul said I've been moved to Sugar House."

Stuart looked as if he was about to explode. "All right. Come on." He strode out of the hotel so fast she almost had to run to keep up with him. Once outside, he stuffed her into the Jeep, started the motor and sped up the mountain road toward Sugar House.

"Dammit!" He hit the steering wheel with his open hand. "How could Polly have let her—"

Miranda held on to the sides of her seat and asked, "What's wrong, Stuart?"

"Nothing," he muttered unconvincingly. "Which suite do you suppose Mother christened the Maude Merrick Suite?"

"I don't know," she said. "I've never been there, remember?" But she had a sinking feeling.

Two days later, Miranda glumly paced up and down in her bedroom on the third floor of Sugar House. For all the good it had done her to be in the same house as the safe, she might as well have stayed in Jamaica.

John and Mary Michaels—the honeymoon couple—had yet to emerge from the Maude Merrick suite, which, of course, had turned out to be Maude's old bedroom.

Stuart hadn't played any more games with her—he'd barely spoken to her. He, Polly and Victoria were all busy keeping the resort and the Sugar House annex running smoothly. They'd refused her offer to help—she'd had

visions of playing maid and delivering fresh towels and
sheets to the newlyweds. But no, that wasn't possible,
they'd insisted. She was a guest, after all.

A guest inconvenienced by Island International, Stuart
had said, since she'd been compelled to move twice since
her arrival at San Sebastian. The resort owed her for that,
he'd declared. And since Jamaica, he was sure he knew
exactly what kind of vacation she liked—so he'd scheduled every minute of her day from breakfast to bedtime.

She'd sailed, snorkeled, swum and sunned until she
was as fit as Jane Fonda. She'd only escaped a deep-sea
fishing trip today by pleading an allergy to live bait.

Miranda stopped by the open door to her room and
listened. Even though she was on the floor above them,
she'd be able to hear if the Michaelses finally emerged
from their room. They had to come out soon—no one
could live on love forever! Disgusted, she began pacing
again.

Time was running out. She had to be back in Los An-
geles the first weekend in June. She was going to be
Maude's maid of honor. In spite of having been married
four times, Maude had never had a formal church wedding, and she'd never been married in June. This time,
she said, she was taking no chances—every tradition
concerning weddings and marriage was going to be
faithfully observed.

Miranda's eyes filled up—only because she'd been
thinking about Maude and her superstitious zeal to make
sure this wedding was her last. Not because a certain
gray-eyed devil had studiously ignored her ever since their
precipitous return to San Sebastian.

No, she wasn't crying over Stuart Winslow. What was
there to cry about? Oh, she'd had a few bad moments
when it seemed as though he'd lost interest because he

couldn't get her into his bed, but she'd gotten over that. She couldn't love a man who only wanted one thing from a woman, could she? Of course not. Therefore, Stuart couldn't be that kind of man.

It really was a good thing that he'd left her alone, she told herself. She hadn't had to tell him any more lies, and as soon as she got to the safe, she could tell him everything. Miranda pictured his surprise at finding out about the secret cache of jewels.

He'd be amused at Maude's plot to recover her property, and once she'd explained about her promise, he'd understand why she'd had to keep her relationship to Maude a secret. He might even admire her for keeping her promise. The best part of Miranda's daydream was when Stuart confessed his love for her. She'd tell him she loved him, too, and they'd live happily ever after—and not in a hotel, either.

She had to get those jewels!

It was time for action. No matter what those people in Maude's bedroom were doing, they'd done it long enough. Miranda hurriedly changed into white shorts and shirt and grabbed her tennis racket. She walked down the stairs to the second floor and stopped outside the door to Maude's old bedroom.

A small sign tacked on the door proclaimed the Maude Merrick suite in calligraphy. Grinning, Miranda decided Maude would be pleased. The Stage Door Deli had named a sandwich after her, but as far as Miranda knew, no one had ever named a bedroom after her mother.

She'd raised her hand to knock when a loud, masculine moan sounded from the interior of the suite.

"What are you doing there?"

Miranda whirled around. Stuart was halfway up the stairway. Improvising quickly, she complained, "I was lonesome. And bored. Everyone around here is so busy. I thought I'd introduce myself to the newlyweds."

"If you're bored, why did you miss the deep-sea charter?"

"I didn't miss it—I gave it a pass," she said, smiling at him. So he'd been keeping tabs on her—surely that was a good sign. "I don't care much for deep-sea fishing."

"You should have told me. I'd have arranged something else."

"When? You're never around. Besides, I don't like having every minute of my day scheduled."

"You did when we were in Jamaica."

"That was different," she muttered, then, before he asked, "Do you think the Michaelses would be interested in a game?" Miranda gave her racket a swing.

"Triples?" he asked.

"Don't be sarcastic, Stuart. I was only—"

Another groan emanated from the suite, followed by a feminine squeal.

Stuart's eyebrows shot up. "It sounds like the honeymooners are otherwise occupied."

"In broad daylight?" Miranda blurted.

"Come on, Miranda." He took her by the arm and dragged her away from the door and down the stairway. "You need lessons."

"No, I don't. I've had lots of tennis lessons."

"Not tennis lessons—lessons about the birds and bees." He stopped at the bottom of the stairs and stood directly in front of her. "Honeymooners do not want to play tennis with strangers, Miranda. And why do you think you have to make love in the dark?" He gave her the kind of look that made her pulse race.

Miranda blushed. "I don't think that. I don't," she insisted. "But Polly said Mr. and Mrs. Michaels haven't come out of that room once in over three days. That can't be healthy.''

"I'd say they're very healthy. Especially him. Anyway, the health of our guests isn't your concern."

"I told you—I'm bored. And I wanted to do something to help. You and your mother and Polly are so busy."

"We work here."

"Your mother doesn't."

"She's family. You're a guest."

"Is that all I am to you? Just another guest?"

"I—" He stopped abruptly. "Come on, I'll take you to the resort. You can visit Tommy. Bill and Cathy, too."

"I don't want to intrude on their honeymoon."

"You were going to intrude on the Michaelses."

She glared at him. "Cathy doesn't need any competition for Tommy's affection right now. I'll just stay here and read a book."

"No. I'm taking you to the resort—that's where the tennis courts are. You did plan to play tennis this afternoon, didn't you?" He stared pointedly at her racket.

*No, I planned to crack a safe—after I'd lured the Michaelses out of the suite with promises of a ménage à trois,* she fumed silently as she reluctantly followed Stuart out to the waiting Jeep. Once he'd begun the drive down the hillside, she asked, "Do we still have a date tonight?"

He took his eyes off the road long enough to shoot her a surprised look. "Date? Tonight?"

"It is Saturday, Stuart. Classics Night, remember?"

"I remember that. What I seem to have forgotten is asking you to go with me."

"Well, I can fix that. I'll ask you. Stuart, will you take me to the movies tonight, please?"

He downshifted into a hairpin curve. Once they were on a relatively straight stretch of road, he answered. "All right. I'll take you, on one condition."

"What's that?"

"Promise me you'll leave the newlyweds alone."

"I won't bother them."

"I want your promise."

"You've got it."

"No, I don't. Say the words, Miranda."

"I promise not to bother the newlyweds." She gave him a three-fingered salute. "Scout's honor."

# *Chapter Eight*

Stuart dropped an obviously disgruntled Miranda off at the tennis courts and returned to his office. Sitting down at his desk, he breathed a sigh of relief. His luck was holding—he'd gotten to Sugar House before Miranda had wormed her way into the Maude Merrick suite.

But the close call meant he'd have to reconsider his plan. Keeping Miranda away from the safe by signing her up for every available activity on San Sebastian was not foolproof. The only alternative, as far as he could see, was to keep her occupied himself.

But could he risk that? Miranda had repeatedly proven she could make him lose control. Each time he held her close and looked into those clear blue eyes, he found it that much harder to remember she was Maude Merrick's daughter.

He hadn't wanted to continue his personal surveillance, but if he was going to keep her away from Maude's safe, he would have to keep a close eye on Miranda. He had no choice.

Stuart laughed out loud. Who was he kidding? He wasn't being noble and self-sacrificing. He simply wanted to be with Miranda. It had been hell staying away from her for two days. His smile slipped. What would his life be like after she left San Sebastian?

A knock sounded at the door and Stuart pushed that disturbing thought aside. He rose to greet Victoria as she entered his office. "Hello, Mother."

She smiled at him as she sat down and put a folder on his desk. "Hello, Stuart. I just saw Miranda on the tennis courts. I see I was right in deducing that you must be here if you weren't there with her. I don't understand it, though. Why on earth are you working on such a beautiful day?"

"I have a lot to do."

"Surely nothing that can't wait until Monday. You really shouldn't work every weekend."

"Dad did."

"Yes, you're right about that," she said, not quite keeping the bitterness out of her voice. "And what did he achieve? An early grave."

Ignoring her comment, he sat down and reached for the folder she'd put in front of him. "Looks like I'm not the only one who's been working." He looked up in time to catch her smiling.

"That's different. I'm having fun—more than I've had in years." A look of concern replaced her sheepish grin. "What about you? Are you having fun?"

"Sure I am."

"Are you? Sometimes I think you take your father's legacy much too seriously. But Miranda was changing that, wasn't she?"

Stuart answered her with a negligent shrug. He didn't want to talk about Miranda's effect on him.

"What happened in Jamaica? You've been scowling and growling ever since you got back. Did you and Miranda have a lover's quarrel?"

Tapping his fingers on the desk, Stuart eyed his mother. What was going on? The last time she'd showed an interest in his love life, he'd been in prep school. "We're not lovers, Mother."

"Oh."

"Oh? That's all you've got to say?" It obviously wasn't—she was itching to give him some motherly advice. He could see it in her eyes.

"What do you want me to say? That I'm sorry you and Miranda aren't lovers? All right. I *am* sorry. I think she's good for you. And you seemed to think so, too. Admit it, Stuart, you were enjoying her company, until you came back from Jamaica."

"I was, and we had fun in Jamaica, too, until—"

"Until what?"

"Until I remembered what kind of woman she is."

"What kind is that?"

"The kind I can't afford."

Victoria raised an eyebrow. "Can you afford to lose her? I don't know what happened in Runaway Bay, but—"

"Nothing happened, Mother."

"Then don't waste the few days you have left to be with her."

Stuart grinned. For some reason, his mother's meddling wasn't irritating him like it usually did. This time her fussing at him was kind of cute. "I'm seeing her tonight. She asked me to take her to the movies."

"Good for her." Victoria smiled. "I do admire these modern women who aren't afraid to pursue a man. You did have the sense to accept, I hope."

Stuart started to tell her that having Miranda chase after him didn't mean anything. But it did, he realized. Miranda no longer needed him to get to Sugar House—so if she asked him to escort her to Classics Night it had to be because she wanted to be with him.

Pleased with that insight, Stuart grinned again, then flushed guiltily when he saw that his mother was waiting for his response. "Yeah, I accepted." Wanting to change the subject before she asked any more questions about Miranda, he pointed to the folder. "What are you working on?"

"The menus. I think we should have some low-fat items available."

"People on vacation don't want health food!"

"Some do. Many of our guests—especially the older ones—are paying more attention to things like cholesterol and fat content these days."

"You may be right." He leaned back in his chair and looked at his mother. Ever since she'd handled the overbooking crisis, she'd been different—less self-centered, more energetic.

Of course, she'd given him some bad moments when he'd found out she'd moved them all to Sugar House, but that hadn't been her fault. No reason for her to know he'd break into a cold sweat at the thought of Miranda happily ensconced in her mother's old bedroom—Victoria hadn't known about Maude's safe. "You really are having a good time working, aren't you?"

"Yes." She smiled at him. "I'd forgotten how much I enjoyed working with your father—at the beginning, when he needed my help. For a while we were a team."

His father hadn't built his empire single-handed, after all. Miranda had guessed as much. "Why did you stop?"

"Robert was old-fashioned. He thought I shouldn't have to work, that the man should be the sole breadwinner. When he could afford to pay someone to do what I'd been doing, he decided he wanted a wife who was a possession, not a partner. And I wasn't modern enough to challenge him."

Stuart raised his eyebrows. That was a view of his parents' marriage he'd never seen before. He eyed his mother thoughtfully. "How would you feel about a permanent job with Island International?"

Victoria's eyes widened. "I'd love it—if it were a real job and not one made up to keep me happy and out of your hair."

"It's a real job—assistant manager at the Runaway Bay resort. If you want it, you can have it."

"I'll take it," she said briskly. "When do I start?"

He laughed. "Don't you want to know more about your job description? Salary?"

"Details." She dismissed them with a wave of her hand. "I'm too excited to concentrate on details. Besides, I know how well you treat your employees."

"In that case, is Monday too soon?"

"Not at all. I'll go pack." Victoria rose gracefully and walked to the door. She stopped with her hand on the doorknob and looked back at him, her eyes suspiciously bright. "Thank you, Stuart. I'll do a good job for you."

"I know you will, Mother," he said huskily.

"And I'll tell Monarch Hotels that Island International is going to stay a family business."

Swallowing the lump in his throat, Stuart could only smile and nod in response. Family, he thought wonderingly—why hadn't his father taught him that was the most important part of a family business?

Miranda glanced at the clock on the chiffonier. As usual, she'd gotten ready too early. And, as usual, she was looking forward to seeing Stuart with a combination of excitement and apprehension. He'd called her from his office to tell her he'd be by to get her a few minutes before eight. It was barely seven-thirty.

She studied her reflection in the cheval glass and frowned. The cranberry red dress had looked prim on the hanger, with its high neck and softly flared skirt. But she'd been right to think Maude never would have bought prim—the silk jersey clung lovingly to every curve.

It was sexy, all right, but was it too subtle? Her shoulders were bare and the skirt ended several inches above her knees, but maybe she should wear something that showed more skin. She wanted to look so good that Stuart wouldn't even think about ignoring her again.

Miranda turned away from her image and paced the length of her small bedroom wondering which Stuart would be picking her up tonight—the playful lover he'd been that night in Jamaica or the no-nonsense businessman he'd been the next morning?

She continued to pace as she told herself she'd be better off if neither the lover nor the businessman showed up. She should stay at Sugar House tonight—she had a job to do. What if tonight was the night the lovebirds finally emerged from their nest? She wouldn't be here, and all because she'd let her heart overrule her head. She wanted more time with the man she loved.

But did he want to spend time with her? True, he'd agreed to take her to Classics Night, but it had been her idea and he hadn't seemed enthusiastic. And, much as she'd like to forget it, he had avoided her for forty-eight hours.

On the other hand, when she hadn't shown up for the fishing trip, he'd come to check on her. He must have been worried about her. That was a good sign, wasn't it?

Miranda stopped at the window overlooking the rear of Sugar House and stared down at the sparkling blue water in the swimming pool. Face it. She didn't have a clue as to how Stuart felt about her. No amount of fretting would help—not when Stuart persisted in giving off conflicting signals.

Squaring her shoulders, she made a decision. She'd just have to ask him what his intentions were. And she'd do it tonight, after the movie. If there was no chance she'd ever be more than a temporary diversion to him, she needed to know, the sooner the better. She would be leaving San Sebastian in a few days, and if she had to leave her heart behind, she would survive.

People got over broken hearts—look at Maude.

Holding her head high, she went to meet Stuart.

He was waiting for her at the bottom of the stairs. One look and Miranda's pulse began to race. He wasn't wearing a tie and he'd rolled up the sleeves of his shirt, exposing his tan forearms. He didn't look at all businesslike.

She tightened her grip on the railing and walked carefully down the stairs. As she approached the last step, Stuart let out a slow wolf whistle. Startled, Miranda said, "I thought you didn't know how to whistle."

He grinned. "Tommy taught me how—with a little help from Lauren Bacall. 'Pucker up your lips and blow,' remember?"

"I remember." Miranda took his outstretched hand and let him lead her out into the tropical night.

"Wait a minute," Stuart said, tugging on her hand to stop her. He picked a flower the exact color of her dress from a shrub next to the front door and carefully tucked it behind her left ear.

A spicy odor filled Miranda's nostrils as she breathed deeply. She didn't know if the scent came from the flower or Stuart's cologne or a combination of the two, but she knew she'd always remember the exotic smell.

Once they were settled in the Jeep and under way, she asked, "Does it look like Classics Night will be a success?"

"Don't know yet—we don't have advance ticket sales." Stuart turned the wheel and continued, "Raoul did say there have been a lot of inquiries. The theater won't be empty, though. Polly will be there, and some of the other employees."

Miranda brushed a windblown strand of hair from her eyes and slanted a look at Stuart, suddenly glad they wouldn't be alone. The night Stuart had taken her and Tommy to see *Treasure Island,* Tommy had sat between them. Tonight they'd be shoulder to shoulder in the dark intimacy of the quaint theater, a scaled-down replica of one of the ornate theaters built during the golden age of movies.

It would take more than darkness and proximity to overcome her conviction that sex should come after requited love—but it wouldn't hurt to have other people around.

"You didn't mention your mother. Isn't Victoria coming?"

"No." He flashed her a grin. "She's getting ready to go to Runaway Bay. She's the new assistant manager."

"Assistant manager? Oh, Stuart! That's wonderful."

"Yeah, it is." He shook his head in amazement. "Such a simple solution, and if you hadn't suggested Mother might want a job..."

"It would have occurred to you anyway, especially after she handled the problem of the extra guests so well."

"Maybe. Maybe not. First Tommy, now my mother—you've been a real help, Miranda." He reached over and took her hand, lacing his fingers through hers.

A wave of pleasure washed over her. "I'm glad I could be of service," she said, giving him a saucy grin.

Stuart downshifted through the final hairpin curve and a few minutes later he pulled up in front of the theater. Miranda looked up at the marquee where "San Sebastian's own Maude Merrick stars in *Forbidden Love* was written in gilt letters.

When Stuart ushered her into the crowded lobby, Miranda breathed a sigh of relief. She didn't have to worry about being alone with Stuart.

"Popcorn?" asked Stuart, pausing by the refreshment stand.

"No, thank you." She couldn't eat when her mouth felt like it was lined with cotton batting.

After Stuart bought himself a box of popcorn and a soft drink, Miranda started for the entrance to the theater.

"Not that way." His hands full, Stuart nodded his head in the direction of a door off to the side. "This way."

Stuart juggled his popcorn and drink and managed to open the door. He stood aside to let her precede him up the narrow stairway.

"Go on up," said Stuart as she hesitated in the doorway. "The stairs lead to the owner's box."

"Owner's box?" she said faintly as she began to climb the stairs.

"Actually it's more like a private balcony."

She looked at him over her shoulder. "Private? How private? Will Polly be there?"

"No. What's the matter? Afraid to be alone with me?"

Miranda tossed her head and continued up the stairs. "Of course not. I'm surprised you want to be alone with me, that's all. You haven't been very friendly lately."

"I'm sorry—I was spending too much time on business. But tonight I'm all yours."

Miranda reached the top of the stairs, nervously aware of Stuart following close behind her. His last remark had done nothing for her composure. She went through an open doorway at the top of the stairs and discovered the tiny balcony contained four oversize theater chairs in two rows.

She took a seat in the front row. Stuart put his popcorn and drink on the wide railing in front of the chairs and sat down beside her. "Looks like Classics Night is a hit," he said. "The theater's almost full."

"I knew we weren't the only ones who like old movies," she said smugly. The gleam in his eye made her suddenly aware of how isolated they were. Chiding herself for being nervous, Miranda reminded herself they'd been alone in a hotel suite in Jamaica and Stuart had behaved like a gentleman—except for taking off his pants, of course.

But she didn't plan on dumping anything in his lap tonight, so everything should be just fine. She smoothed her skirt and arranged herself in her seat, far enough away that she couldn't be blamed for any tantalizing brushes of thigh against thigh, shoulder against shoulder. If Stuart wanted to play games in the dark, he'd have to make the first move.

"Guess not," he agreed, tossing a kernel of popcorn in his mouth. "What movie would you like to see next week?" He stretched his long legs in front of him and casually draped his arm along the back of her chair.

"I won't be here next week."

"Sure you will. You won Island International's first annual Most Helpful Guest Award—an additional week's stay. Free." Stuart pulled up the armrest between their two seats, reached over and tucked her against him.

"You made that up," she said breathlessly. "There is no Most Helpful Guest Award."

"There is now. We're going to call it the Miranda."

"Stuart, stop teasing."

"I'm not teasing, Miranda," he said, his voice grave. "I want you to stay."

Miranda's heart slammed against her ribs. "I can't. I wish I could, but I can't."

"Why not? Did you get another job?"

"No, but I have a prior commitment."

"Commitment?" Stuart's brows came together in a forbidding scowl. "Daniel what's-his-name?"

"No, of course not. A wedding. I'm going to be the maid of honor at a wedding."

The theater lights dimmed. "We'll talk more about this later," he said, reaching for his popcorn.

The flickering images on the silver screen began to work their magic. Miranda had almost relaxed when Stuart held the popcorn box in front of her.

"Have some," he whispered.

Miranda, engrossed in the film, mechanically took a handful and munched.

Stuart chuckled. "I knew you'd want some—that's why I bought a large box."

Miranda swallowed and grinned sheepishly. "How did you know?" she asked.

"No real movie fan could sit through a feature film without popcorn."

She reached for another handful of popcorn and got Stuart's hand instead. "I thought you'd had enough."

"I have, but I want to feed you." He touched her lips with a buttery kernel. Miranda's mouth opened automatically and she took the popcorn into her mouth, but Stuart kept his fingers on her lips.

"Lick," he ordered softly. "You left the butter behind."

Miranda sucked in her breath. "I can't lick."

"No guts?"

"No spit."

Stuart laughed out loud. "Dry mouth?"

"Like the Sahara."

"I can take care of that." He leaned over and retrieved the soda and gave it to her.

Miranda took several large swallows of the icy drink. She needed cooling off. When she'd finished, Stuart took the empty cup from her nerveless fingers. He put it and the popcorn box on the floor.

Stuart touched his lips to hers, the gentle kiss enough to make her heart beat faster. She sighed against his mouth as his tongue traced the outline of her lips, and shivered when he boldly thrust his tongue into the moist interior of her mouth.

"Mmm," he said, licking his lips. "You taste good—like popcorn and woman."

Conversation ceased as Stuart kissed his way from her temple to her throat. When his hand moved from her shoulder to her breast, Miranda gently pushed him away. "Watch the movie, Stuart," she ordered softly.

"No more kisses?" he whispered in her ear. His warm breath on her neck gave her goose bumps.

"No." She folded her hands in her lap and refused to look at him, afraid she'd give in to the desire to return to his arms.

"We don't have much time left, Miranda. Not if you're leaving in a few days."

"Shh." Keeping her eyes glued to the movie screen, she tried to concentrate on the film. Time passed and the movie's images danced in front of her, but Miranda couldn't get Stuart's kisses out of her mind.

"This is my favorite part," she told him.

Studying the screen, Miranda watched as Tynan, playing the part of wealthy financier Philip Chase, entered the humble home of poor-but-honest Elizabeth Sherill, played by Maude.

Startled by Philip's reflection in her mirror, Elizabeth turned to face him. "Philip! What are you doing here? I never expected to see you again after... after..."

"After you slapped my face and told me what I could do with my offer to make you my mistress?" Philip laughed ruefully.

Elizabeth modestly lowered her eyes and nodded. Philip pulled her into his arms and gazed deeply into her eyes.

"I've come for you, Elizabeth. I had to. You took my heart with you when you left Maracaibo, and now I find I have need of it."

"You do? What for?" Elizabeth asked, her voice trembling with emotion.

"So that I can love you, my darling."

"You love me?" Elizabeth's turquoise eyes filled with tears.

"Yes, I love you. More than my life. For all my life. Say you'll be my wife, my darling."

"Oh, Philip. I do love you so! I'd be proud to be your wife."

The on-screen lovers kissed passionately while the music reached a crescendo. The scene faded to black and the lights in the theater came up just as the words The End appeared on the screen.

Miranda sobbed.

"Don't cry, honey. It's only a movie." Stuart reached in his pocket and handed her his handkerchief.

"I-I'm s-sorry." Miranda blew her nose noisily. "I can't help it. That scene always makes me cry."

Stuart put his arms around her and gave her a hug. "Why, sweetheart? It's pure corn."

"I know that." She gulped, choking back a sob. "It's just that, after my p-parents were divorced, when I'd watch that scene, I'd dream of my father coming after us, like Philip comes after Elizabeth in the movie. Only he n-never did." She buried her face against Stuart's shoulder.

His arms tightened around her. "Poor Miranda. I never would have shown *Forbidden Love* if I'd known what it meant to you. You should have told me."

"But Stuart," she whimpered, "I'm glad you chose it. It's my favorite m-movie."

He used one finger to trace the path of a tear down her cheek. "God, Miranda, you're beautiful," he whispered.

"Oh, sure. With my eyes red and my face splotchy from crying." She laughed weakly.

"You're beautiful anyway, but that's not what I meant. I think it's beautiful that you care so much for—"

She looked at him expectantly, her lips curved in a tiny smile. "For what?"

"Corny old movies," he finished lamely. "Are you all right now?"

"I'm through blubbering, if that's what you mean."

"Let's go home."

During the short trip to Sugar House Miranda wanted to tell him that it wasn't only the ending of the movie that had made her cry—it was also the thought of leaving him. But if she told him that, he might ask her to stay again, and then what would she do?

She wanted to stay, but not for only another week. She wanted longer—fifty or sixty years. But she couldn't tell him that.

Stuart parked the Jeep and helped her out. "Penny for your thoughts," he said as they walked into the house.

"They're not worth that," she said miserably.

He tilted up her chin and scrutinized her face. "Still sad because of the movie?"

"No. Yes. Not exactly."

"Want to explain that answer?" he asked dryly.

She shook her head.

Stuart took her arm and walked her up the stairs to her room. At her door, he took her in his arms and gave her a chaste kiss on the forehead. "Get some sleep, Miranda. We'll talk tomorrow."

He turned and walked into his room across the hall, closing the door behind him.

Miranda undressed and put on a short silk nightshirt, but she knew she was too keyed up to sleep. Why hadn't she told Stuart she wanted to talk to him tonight?

No guts, she answered herself with a disgusted snort. She was afraid it was too late to tell him the truth. Once he knew she'd lied to him, he'd never fall in love with her—not in the few days she had left on his island.

With a melancholy sigh, she went to the window and pulled back the lace curtains. The pool lights had been turned off, but the full tropical moon was making a silver trail across the surface of the swimming pool. The thought of the silky cool water was too tempting to ignore. Strenuous exercise would make her sleepy. After a good night's rest, she'd stop wimping around and tell Stuart exactly who she was and why she'd come to San Sebastian.

And she'd take all the time she needed to make him fall in love with her, once Maude and Tynan were safely married again.

Feeling better than she had in days, Miranda stripped off her nightshirt and donned her red bikini. Grabbing a towel, she headed for the pool.

# *Chapter Nine*

A floorboard creaked outside of his room and Stuart went to investigate. He opened the door in time to see Miranda, dressed in her red bikini, tiptoeing down the stairs. He grinned, glad to discover that she couldn't sleep, either. He'd considered a swim himself, but had opted for a cold shower, instead.

If he'd known they'd both be victims of insomnia, he wouldn't have ended the evening so soon. It had taken every ounce of willpower to walk away from her when all he'd wanted was to take her in his arms. He'd planned to let her have her way with him, after all. She owed him for all she'd put him through. And letting her make love to him was a way to get even with her for lying to him.

He couldn't take advantage of her now.

After *Forbidden Love*, Miranda had seemed so vulnerable, so sweet. Not at all like the scheming seductress he'd made her out to be. She had cried. Real tears. And it had been his fault for showing that movie.

Stuart cursed under his breath. Even if he'd forgotten the melodramatic ending, he should have realized watching the only movie her parents had made together might upset her. Seeing her reaction, listening to her explain her dream of her parents' reconciliation, had forced him to think about how hard it must have been for her to grow up with those two larger-than-life people.

No wonder she'd opted for a career in the audience instead of on-screen. She must have realized early on that if she became an actress, she'd risk unfavorable comparisons with her illustrious parents. Miranda wouldn't have been a very good actress, anyway. She didn't know how to lie.

How did Maude and Tynan feel about their daughter? Had they expected her to follow in their footsteps? Were they disappointed in her?

Robert Winslow had always made it clear he expected his son to take over the business. Luckily, he'd been able to meet every challenge his father had thrown at him. Stuart knew how he would have felt if he hadn't been able to do what his father had asked of him. He'd have felt like a failure.

Right now, he felt like a rat for choosing to screen *Forbidden Love*—for the express purpose of shaking Miranda's composure. But he hadn't anticipated her tears, or the fierce protectiveness he'd felt when she'd turned to him for comfort.

Stepping into his room, Stuart paced the floor. At least he hadn't been callous enough to remark on her resemblance to a young Maude. He'd actually planned to do that—another attempt to force her into admitting the relationship. Stuart groaned. He didn't want to force her into anything. He wanted Miranda to tell him the truth willingly.

And who was he to blame her for continuing her charade when he wasn't ready to confess his sins? The truth was, he didn't want her to know that he was a thief. She might never have to know if he could convince the bank to release its collateral a few months early. There was a good chance he could do that. Now that he and his mother were on the same side Monarch was no longer a threat. They could offer the bank their combined stock in Island International as collateral for the loan in lieu of Maude's jewels.

But he needed time to negotiate with the bankers—a week at least. He'd thought he could convince Miranda to stay a few days more, especially since she hadn't gotten the jewels yet. It had never occurred to him that she would have a prior commitment.

He stopped pacing and stared blankly at the seascape hanging over the fireplace mantel. Whose wedding was it, anyway? Much-married Maude leapt to mind, but it couldn't be her. He hadn't seen anything in the papers about Maude snaring a fifth husband.

Stuart shoved a hand through his hair. It didn't matter *why* Miranda had to leave San Sebastian—her leaving was what mattered.

He snapped his fingers. The problem wasn't insurmountable. All he had to do was ask Miranda to come back to San Sebastian after she'd attended the wedding—he'd add a return ticket to the prize for Most Helpful Guest. She'd come back—she'd have to, for the jewels if nothing else.

Rummaging through the dresser drawers, Stuart found his swimsuit and put it on. A midnight swim with Miranda was too tempting to resist. Why waste a golden opportunity to give her another reason to come back to San Sebastian—him.

* * *

Miranda floated on her back, gazing at the countless stars in the midnight sky. A languid movement of her hands was enough to keep her afloat in the cocooning warmth of the water. She'd swum enough laps to make herself pleasantly drowsy, but couldn't work up the energy to get out of the pool.

And she wasn't sure if she'd sleep, no matter how tired she was. She couldn't stop thinking about Stuart. He was giving her conflicting signals again. Why had he asked her to stay another week, then left her at her door with a kiss that could only be described as brotherly? Oblivious to her surroundings, she yawned and swallowed a mouthful of pool water. Sputtering and flailing her arms, Miranda jerked out of her floating position and sank.

Miranda came up gasping and choking and found herself eye to eye with Stuart.

"Are you all right?" he asked, pounding her on the back.

She nodded as she tried to stand. Miranda promptly went under again. She'd forgotten they were in the deep end of the pool. Stuart grabbed her by the waist and lifted her up.

Miranda braced her hands on his shoulders to steady herself while she caught her breath. "I'm in over my head," she told him, her voice weak—and not from her dunking. Underwater, her legs were tangling with Stuart's, sending shock waves through her body.

"I know the feeling," he muttered, treading water. "Hang on, honey. I'll take care of you." He wrapped one arm securely around her, leaned back and began a slow backstroke to the shallow end of the pool.

"I know how to swim, Stuart," she said, trying unsuccessfully to wiggle away from him.

"You went under twice," he pointed out, bumping against the side of the pool. Stuart rested his shoulders against the tiles and let his lower body drift up to meet hers floating on the surface of the water.

"I wasn't in any danger of drowning." She made herself slide off his body, finding the slick heat of his naked skin against hers much too disturbing. Bobbing up and down in the chest-deep water, she eyed him warily.

"You mean I didn't just save your life?" Stuart asked. He moved toward her through the water, making tiny waves lap against her sensitized breasts like lover's kisses.

"No, of course not." She began an awkward dog paddle away from him, but found herself reined in by his hand on her waist. Yielding to his gentle tug, she slipped through the water until she was in his arms.

"Darn." His eyes went to her mouth. "And here I thought I'd found a way to be your hero."

"You want to be my hero?"

"Yeah. I do." His arms tightened around her and her breasts flattened against the wall of his chest. Miranda clung to his shoulders as his mouth claimed hers in a breath-stealing kiss.

"I think I'm going under for the third time." Miranda sighed when he finally released her lips.

Stuart trailed kisses from her earlobe to her chin, leaving pleasurable tingles everywhere his lips and tongue touched her skin. "So beautiful," he said, lifting her so that his mouth could taste the swell of her breasts.

"Let me see you, Miranda. I need to see the moonlight on every inch of your skin," he groaned, fumbling with the ties of the bikini top. When it floated away, he tilted her back across one arm and looked down at her, his eyes smoky with desire.

Instinctively, she arched her body, giving Stuart free access to the tender flesh he'd exposed. When his hands and then his mouth found her naked breasts, the sensations his mouth evoked intensified until they were almost painful.

Miranda turned her head into the hollow of his neck. She used her tongue to follow the path of a drop of water from his jaw to his chest. When she found the masculine nipple buried in crisp, black curls, she sucked gently.

A rumble from deep in Stuart's throat let her know her efforts were appreciated. Wanting to please him as much as he was pleasing her, Miranda boldly trailed a hand down his chest, stopping to explore the indentation in his abdomen before moving lower.

"Miranda—"

A square of light spilled onto the water. Startled, Miranda looked up. "Stuart," she hissed. "They're watching us."

"What?" He turned his head and followed her gaze to the window of the Maude Merrick honeymoon suite. Shadows on the curtains clearly outlined two human forms.

"Damn!" Quickly pulling Miranda against him, he concealed her nudity with his body.

Embarrassed, Miranda buried her head against his chest as Stuart carried her out of the pool and into the shadows. Reaching down, he snagged a towel from one of the lounges as he headed for the French doors.

The light in the window disappeared as suddenly as it had appeared. "They're gone." she said. "We could go back and...swim some more." Miranda bit her lip and hoped her blushes didn't show in the moonlight—she hadn't meant to sound quite so wanton.

"No. They turned off the light, but they could still be watching." Stuart put her down and wrapped the towel around her sarong fashion. He tucked in the ends of the towel, his fingers lingering against her breasts. "We'd better go in."

"You're probably right," she agreed, disappointed.

Stuart hurried her up the stairs, past the honeymooners' suite, not stopping until they were outside her room.

He opened the door, and Miranda stepped inside. Sensing that he wasn't following her, she turned. He was standing in the doorway.

"Good night, Miranda," he said.

"Good night?" He couldn't leave her now—not after he'd reduced her to a mass of quivering sensation. She wanted more of those bone-melting caresses. "But I thought... aren't you... Don't you want to..."

"Yes, I want to, and no, I'm not going to. Not tonight, anyway. Heroes don't take advantage of innocents. I'm trying to be your hero, remember?"

Miranda shoved her wet hair out of her face and stared at him. "Innocent? You've been acting like you thought I was some kind of mantrap."

"I did think that at first. But only an innocent would try to seduce a man by imitating movie stars. A real temptress would rely on personal experience."

"Oh?" Miranda moved closer to Stuart and looked at him through half-closed eyes. "When did you come to that conclusion?" she asked, her voice throaty with frustrated desire.

"I got a glimmer of the truth when you started being yourself with Tommy. When you turned skittish in Jamaica—that was the final clue."

"What did you mean, imitations?"

"I recognized Marilyn Monroe and Lauren Bacall. I am a fan, remember."

"Do you think I'm tempting when I'm being myself?" she asked, running her hands over the hard muscles of his chest. When she lifted her arms to his shoulders, the towel began to slip.

A silver gleam flared in Stuart's eyes as he grabbed the towel and tucked it more tightly around her. "You're very tempting, Miranda."

"I'm glad you think so, because—" Miranda tightened her arms around his neck and pressed her breasts against his chest.

"Because?" Stuart's voice was husky.

"I love you," she blurted. She rolled her eyes as she felt the blood rush to her cheeks. "I can't believe I told you that. I meant to wait—" Stepping out of his embrace, she clutched the towel to keep it from falling again. She'd meant to wait until she could tell him who she was.

Stuart pulled her into his arms and gave her a hug. "I'm glad you didn't. Now get some sleep and we'll talk about this tomorrow."

"Can't we talk now?" She didn't want to wait another minute to tell him the truth.

"Not when we're both half-naked. I'm not that good at this hero business yet." He dropped a quick kiss on her parted lips. "Get some sleep, Miranda. And promise me you won't do anything drastic before morning."

"Like what? Coming to your room later, maybe?"

"Don't do it, Miranda. A man can only stand so much. And we need to have a serious talk before we take that step." He pushed her through her open door and closed it.

As soon as the door shut, Miranda did a little dance in the middle of her room. Stuart wanted to be her hero.

Nothing ambiguous about that—it could only mean he was in love with her. And he wanted to have a serious talk. A proposal of marriage was very serious.

"My hero," she sighed, picking up the towel and shimmying out of her bikini bottom.

Using the towel to dry her hair, Miranda ignored the tiny voice that persisted in pointing out Stuart hadn't actually said he loved her. But hadn't Maude told her that some men had trouble saying those three little words?

Miranda found her nightshirt and slipped it on. Jumping into the bed, she fluffed her pillow, arranged the sheet over her and tried to relax. The sooner she slept, the sooner it would be tomorrow.

But how could she sleep when her eyes kept popping open and her mouth wouldn't stop grinning? She turned over and punched her pillow. And that noisy splashing in the pool wasn't helping, either.

Splashing? Electrified, Miranda sat up. Had Stuart gone back to the pool? She leapt out of bed and went to the window. It wasn't Stuart. A man and woman were cavorting in the pool. The honeymooners! It had to be them. She and Stuart must have given them ideas.

She turned toward the bed, then stopped. This was no time to sleep! This was what she'd been waiting for—the Maude Merrick suite was vacant, for a while at least. She peeked through the curtains again. For a good while, she decided.

She rummaged through her purse until she found her key chain. It had a tiny penlight attached, as well as the key Maude had given her. Quietly, she opened her door and inched across the hardwood floor to the stairway, then crept down the stairs. Miranda winced when she stepped on a tread that creaked. She paused, holding her breath for what seemed like a full minute. Nothing.

She let her breath out and continued down the stairs. Miranda was relieved to see the door to the honeymoon suite was slightly ajar. Somehow, pushing it open seemed less of an intrusion than if she'd had to unlock it.

She entered the suite and closed the door behind her. Standing with her back against the wall, she waited for her racing pulse to slow.

The moon shining through the lace-curtained windows gave enough light for her to see the fireplace. She took one last calming breath and headed for the hearth.

"Second stone from the wall," she muttered, kneeling down and touching it. The stone came up easily and then—finally—she was looking at the safe.

Her heart pounding in her ears, Miranda switched on the penlight. "One left, five right, forty-nine left," she whispered as she turned the dial. She twisted the handle to the safe and pulled it open. Miranda reached inside. Nothing. She felt around again.

Empty! The safe was empty.

Impossible, she thought, staring in disbelief into the black hole. Suddenly a hand closed over her mouth and she was roughly jerked to her feet. She tried to scream, but her cry was muffled by a large male hand. Struggling frantically, she managed to twist her head around and froze when she saw her assailant. Stuart. She slumped against him. For one heart-stopping moment, she'd thought it was Mr. Michaels.

"Don't say a word," Stuart ordered, his voice cold. He took his hand away from her mouth, but before she could even nod her agreement, he tossed her over his shoulder and carried her up the stairs. He didn't put her down until they were inside his bedroom with the door closed.

Her legs trembling from the aftermath of shock, Miranda sat down on the bed. "Someone stole the jewels.

Stuart, there were jewels in that safe, valuable jewels. We have to call the police."

"We don't need the police." Stuart loomed over her, scowling. Dressed only in a pair of jeans, his feet and chest bare, he looked furious. The moonlight and shadows made his face a series of hard angles. The mouth that had kissed her so tenderly was now thinned into an angry line. "Unless you're ready to go to jail."

She held her hands out beseechingly. "I can explain, Stuart," she said, unable to keep the fear out of her voice. "I'm not a jewel thief. I'm not who you think I am. That is, I am, but you don't know who I—"

"You're Maude's daughter." His words were clipped.

"Yes, I am," she said, surprised. "I would have told you sooner, but—"

"You wanted to get her jewels first."

"You knew who I was? Why I was here?" A sick feeling knotted her stomach. She lowered her eyes, then looked up at him again. "How long have you known?"

"From the beginning. Polly recognized your name on the yacht's passenger list."

"Why didn't you tell me?"

"Why didn't *you* tell *me?*" he countered.

Miranda looked into gray eyes as cold and hard as steel. She shuddered as an icy chill ran down her spine, and she hastened to explain. "I wanted to tell you, but I couldn't. I promised Maude."

"Ah, yes. And you always keep your promises, don't you?" Stuart scoffed.

Her chin came up. "Yes. I do."

"What about your promise to me? You said you'd stay out of the honeymooners' suite."

"I did not. I promised not to bother them and I didn't. I waited until they were gone before I—"

"Before you broke into their room? What if they'd come back and found you instead of me?"

"I would have explained about the safe and Maude's jewels." The fact that Stuart was at least as guilty of deception as she was finally sank in, and righteous anger began to smolder in her breast. "How did you know about the safe, anyway?"

"The locksmith who installed it told me about it and gave me the combination."

"And the jewels? Do you know what happened to them?"

"I took them."

"Where are they?" she demanded.

"In a bank vault."

Miranda's anger dissolved in a sigh of relief. She stood up. "I guess it wouldn't have been a good idea to leave them in a vacant house. But why didn't you just send them back to Maude?"

"I didn't put Maude's jewels in a bank for safety reasons."

"Then why—"

"I needed money. I used Maude's jewelry to get it." His lips curled in a sardonic grin. "It seemed only fair, since it was her premarital contract that caused the problem."

"You sold Maude's jewels?"

Stuart shook his head. "I used the jewels as collateral for a loan." He began pacing the room like a caged lion.

"Loan?" she said to his back. "You borrowed money?"

He reached the windows and turned to face her. "A lot of money," he said, narrowing his eyes to silver slits.

"Why would you need to do that?" She waved her arm. "You own all this."

Stuart laughed, but the sound held no mirth. "Did you think I was rich, Miranda?" He stopped pacing and pinned her with his gaze. "Is that why you told me you loved me?"

"Don't start that gold-digger business again." Miranda stalked to the end of the room and back. She stopped in front of him, her hands on her hips. "I don't care if you're rich or poor. Just tell me what's going on."

"It's very simple. I needed money to buy Maude's shares. I used her jewels to get it. They're being held as collateral by the bank."

"You used my mother's jewels to borrow money? But Stuart, that's stealing."

"That's right. I'm a thief." He bit out the words through clenched teeth.

Dazed, Miranda shook her head. "No, you can't be. Maude said you were an honest man. If you give the jewels back right away—"

"I can't do that. I won't have the money to pay off the loan for another couple of months. I'd thought about asking the bank to let me substitute Island International stock for the jewels, but I decided against that."

"Why?"

"If something happens and I can't make the final balloon payment, the bank could foreclose—I'd lose the family business. I'm not going to take that risk. Maude will get her jewels back when the loan is paid off."

"That's not good enough. Those jewels are too important to Maude. She calls them her security, her retirement fund. You have to give them back now."

Stuart snaked a hand around her nape and used his other hand to tilt up her chin. "They can't be that important to her, not if she forgot about them for over a year," he said defensively.

"She didn't forget them. She thought they were safe because no one knew where they were. Give them back, Stuart," Miranda pleaded. "You have to."

"I don't have to do anything. You forget—on San Sebastian, I'm the law. Besides, I thought you loved me," he said in a soft, mocking voice. "If you love me, you'll ask Maude to let me keep them."

A sharp pain knifed beneath her left breast. It's true, she thought. Hearts break.

"What's wrong, Miranda?" He sneered. "Not willing to do a little favor for the man you love?"

"I don't do favors for people who use me to get to my parents. Maude was right to cast you as the villain in this melodrama. You're no hero. If you want something from her, ask her yourself."

Stuart's brows snapped together in a fearsome scowl. He turned his back on her and crashed his fist into the wall. "Get out, Miranda," he snarled. "Out of this room and out of my life."

Two weeks later, Stuart opened the red leather case two heavily armed guards had just delivered to his office. Diamonds, rubies and emeralds sparkled and gleamed as he spilled the contents on to his desk. Absently fingering a sapphire and diamond bracelet, Stuart was not surprised he felt none of the seductive pull the fabulous treasure trove should have invoked. He hadn't felt anything since the night he found Miranda kneeling in front of the empty safe.

He'd known why she'd come to San Sebastian. But seeing her frantic search for the missing jewels had shown him, as nothing else had, that she had only one reason for being on his island. She'd never loved him. Ah, well. He didn't need her love. He had his empire.

"Rocks," he said, letting the bracelet slide through his fingers. "Nothing but a bunch of pretty rocks."

He replaced the jewels in their case and walked to the window. The sight of the resort spread out before him didn't cheer him as it had in the past. He supposed he was glad he'd saved it—for his mother, for Polly and the other employees—but he knew now he could have survived without Island International. He walked to his desk. At least having the resorts gave him something to do with the rest of his life. If he worked real hard, he might be able to survive without Miranda.

He laughed, but his laugh had a hollow ring. He'd called Miranda a gold digger, but he was the one who'd always wanted money and the power that came with it. It was the way his father had taught him to measure success. Miranda had tried to teach him a better way.

Love. Family. Fun.

Why hadn't he learned what was really important before it was too late?

# Chapter Ten

"Dearly beloved, we are gathered here today..."

A tear slid down Miranda's cheek. It felt good to cry—her face ached from keeping a smile on for Maude and Tynan. After the years she'd waited for them to rediscover their love for one another, she wasn't about to let her misery spoil their happiness. But it was all right to cry at weddings.

"Wilt thou have this woman..."

Maude looked more beautiful than she ever had, Miranda thought, trying to concentrate on the ceremony. The ivory lace suit she'd chosen to wear was the epitome of understated elegance. And Tynan in white tie and tails had to be the most attractive man in the world.

Except for one.

"With this ring, I thee wed..."

Miranda sniffed and tried to smile. She wouldn't think about...him. Not here. Not today. Stuart Winslow and weddings didn't go together. Just like the two of them

didn't go together. It was no use visualizing her and
Stuart together at the altar repeating the same vows
Maude and Tynan were speaking. Some fantasies were
too painful to indulge in.

"I pronounce that they are man and wife..."

The tears were coming faster now. Miranda squeezed
her eyes shut, wishing they would wash away her mem-
ories of Stuart.

A week later, Miranda slumped down so that her neck
rested on the back of the plush theater chair in Tynan's
small private theater. She reached for the bowl of popcorn on the seat next to her as the opening credits of
*Forbidden Love* scrolled across the screen.

Give in to it, she ordered herself. Wallowing in self-pity
and misery was the order of the day. Maybe the week.
Maybe even the month.

However long it took, she had to get Stuart and her
miserable unrequited love for him out of her system.
Preferably before Maude and Tynan got back from Ta-
hiti. They had been too engrossed with each other to pay
much attention to her before the wedding. Even so, Miranda was almost sure Maude had begun to suspect she'd
left more than the jewels behind when she'd departed
from San Sebastian.

Maude was right to be suspicious. Her trip to San Sebastian, meeting Tommy and his family, falling in love
with Stuart, all those things had changed her. Now she
knew why a career had never been that important to her.
She wanted love and marriage—preferably one love, one
marriage, several children. She had never dared to want
that before. With a mother like Maude, she'd been sure
her dream of a family that lasted forever was genetically
doomed.

Miranda sighed. Wanting wasn't getting. She ought to spend some effort looking for a new job before Maude and Tynan returned to California. She had to do something with her life. Maybe she could find a film collection that specialized in tragedies. She certainly didn't feel like laughing.

She did manage a watery smile as she recalled her last conversation with Maude before she and Tynan had left for the airport.

"Are you sure you don't want to go with us, sweety?" Maude had asked anxiously.

Miranda had snorted. "On your honeymoon? I'm sure."

"But darling, I hate to leave you alone." Maude turned to face her. "Especially now, when you're at loose ends."

"I'll be fine." She gave her mother a hug. "You and Dad have a wonderful time and don't even think about me."

"I can't promise that—you're my other love, after all. And ever since you got back from San Sebastian, you've been . . . different."

"Different?" Miranda nervously averted her eyes, sure that Maude would see the misery there.

"Yes. Sort of preoccupied. You're not feeling bad because you didn't get the jewels, are you?"

"Well, the trip was a failure—"

Maude put a finger on Miranda's lips. "It was not. I'll get the jewels back eventually. And Tynan did give me the earrings and the bracelet to go with my new diamond necklace. He wouldn't have, if I'd had all my jewels before the wedding."

Laughing, Miranda hugged her mother. "You're wonderful."

Maude smiled smugly. "I know. But I like to hear it. Compliments are almost as good as diamonds and rubies."

"Are the jewels still so important, Mother?"

"I'm afraid so. You know insecurity is our curse, sweety."

Miranda gave Maude a puzzled look. "Insecurity? What do you mean?"

"We both have trouble believing a man could love us for ourselves. Remember that lawyer? What was his name?"

"Daniel Eberhart. He didn't make me feel insecure."

"Oh, but he did. The minute you had reason to suspect his motives, you dropped him."

"Daniel didn't want me, he wanted to be Tynan's attorney."

"Maybe he wanted that and you. Did you ever ask him?"

"No. Should I have?"

"If you loved him. You didn't, did you?"

Miranda shook her head. She'd never loved any man before Stuart.

"Well, then, you should have let him go. I hope when you do fall in love you have enough sense to know when you're loved in return. You know, Miranda, before this time with your father, I always felt the men I fell in love with wanted something more than love from me—my aura of glamour, success, that kind of thing. And, since I wasn't sure of their love, I made them pay for what they got with material things. I needed one or the other to feel secure."

"But you know Daddy loves you—"

"Yes. So maybe I won't need diamonds and pearls anymore." Maude patted Miranda on the hand. "But don't tell Tynan that. He won't know what to get me for Christmas if you do.''

Miranda smiled. "It will be our little secret."

"Don't tell Stuart how I feel, either. He should at least feel a little guilty about what he did." A tiny frown wrinkled Maude's brow. "When I think about him stealing my jewels—and I thought he was so honest."

Miranda's smile faded. "He had a good reason, Mother. All those employees."

"Humph. So you said. Taking my jewels was still a rotten thing for him to do." Maude grinned wickedly. 'To tell you the truth, I would have done the same thing, if I'd been in his shoes."

"It was nice of you to write and tell him he could keep them until he paid off the loan."

"You didn't give me much choice—painting that pitiful picture of what would happen to Aunt Polly and the other employees if I jerked the collateral out from under Stuart. Have you mailed the letter yet?"

Miranda nodded. "This morning."

Blinking, Miranda pulled her thoughts back to the present and grabbed a handful of popcorn. That was a week ago. Stuart must have received Maude's letter by now. Would he answer it? Or would he wait until he'd paid off the loan to correspond with Maude about the return of her jewels?

She wanted him to bring the jewels to Beverly Hills himself. If she could see him one more time, she would do what Maude advised. She'd ask him why he'd done what he did. She wouldn't assume his only motive had been to get her to help him keep Maude's jewels—even if he hadn't written or called her since she'd left his island.

Raising her chin, she made a promise to herself. If he didn't come, if he sent the jewels by courier, she'd go to

San Sebastian and make him tell her to her face that he'd only been using her. She had to know for sure that he didn't love her, or she would spend years regretting it.

She crunched the popcorn noisily and turned her attention to the movie. When the final credits rolled, she was crying lustily and didn't realize someone had joined her in the screening room until a handkerchief was shoved in her hand.

"Thanks." She sobbed as she hit the switch that turned on the lights. "Stuart! What are you doing here?" Her heart pounded frantically as she looked at him.

He held up a briefcase. "I came to return Maude's jewels."

"She's not here. She and Tynan left on their honeymoon a week ago."

"I know. Agnes told me that—and where to find you."

Standing up, Miranda reached for the briefcase. When Stuart gave it to her, she avoided his eyes. Maude was right. She was insecure, too insecure to ask the man she loved if he loved her, too afraid the answer would be no. "Well, thank you for returning Maude's jewelry," she said stiffly. "She'll be pleased."

"I'm sorry I missed her. I wanted to thank her for not prosecuting me for theft."

Her gaze flew to his eyes. "Maude never would have done that—she's not that kind of person. And she did write you a letter giving you permission to use her jewelry as collateral."

"Did she? I didn't know."

"You didn't? I...it was mailed the day they left town."

"Did you ask her to write it? It seems a little out of character for the Maude I know."

"I asked, but she would have done it anyway. I think. She's not completely heartless." Miranda turned her gaze away from him and focused on the blank screen. "She's really a very generous person. She's always doing things for people."

"Not for everyone. She does things for you. You thought I was using you to get to Maude, didn't you?"

Lifting her chin, she looked him in the eyes. "You wouldn't have been the first person to do that."

"I didn't mean to, Miranda. But I felt so guilty about taking something that didn't belong to me. I got defensive, and lashed out at you. Can you ever forgive me?"

Miranda dabbed at her eyes with his handkerchief. "Yes." Was that all he wanted? Forgiveness?

"I wanted to thank you, too. For what you did for me and Mother. She's been promoted to manager at the Runaway Bay resort, by the way."

He was grateful, too, it seemed. Swallowing the lump in her throat, Miranda said, "I'm glad Victoria is happy. How's Polly?"

"She's fine. She and Mother loaned me the money to redeem Maude's jewels a month early."

"That was nice of them. But it wasn't necessary."

"Yes, it was. I couldn't wait any longer."

"To be an honest man again?"

He shook his head slowly. "Guess again." He had a mischievous gleam in his eyes.

"I don't feel like playing guessing games, Stuart." If he didn't leave soon, she was going to make a complete fool of herself.

"But we have such a good time when we play games. And you are the one who taught me how."

She shrugged. "Did I? I don't remember."

"Liar. I think you remember every minute you spent on my island. I know I do. I can't forget you, so . . ."

Her heart was beating so loudly she was sure he must hear it. "So? What are you going to do?"

Stuart pulled her out of her seat and into his arms. "I've come for you, Miranda. I had to. You took my heart with you when you left San Sebastian, and now I find I have need of it."

Eying him suspiciously, she asked, "Are you quoting from *Forbidden Love?*"

"Yes. Don't you like my acting?"

Her heart began to beat faster as hope curled through her veins. "You said that dialogue was corny," she reminded him.

"It is. But appropriate for a man in love."

"Is that what you are?" she asked, her mouth curving into a silly grin.

"In spades." His arms opened and she walked into them.

"Good. Now you can tell me why you need your heart back."

"So that I can love you, my darling."

"You love me?"

"Yes, I love you. More than my life. For all my life. Say you'll be my wife, my darling."

"Oh, Stuart. I do love you so! I'd be proud to be your wife."

"You love me, Miranda?" he asked. "After all I've done, do you still love me?"

Miranda tilted her head to one side and looked up at him. "What movie is that from?"

He gave her a gentle shake. "Don't tease, Miranda. Do you love me?"

"I love you," she assured him, wrapping her arms around him.

Stuart let out an exultant yell and swung Miranda around. Putting her down, he kissed her hard and fast. "Now that we've got that settled, I have one more question."

All her love shining in her eyes, she asked, "What?"

"You do know how this movie's going to end, don't you?" he asked huskily, lowering his head to hers.

Miranda smiled. "Happily ever after, of course."

# Epilogue

Maude Merrick swept into the room carrying a box of disposable diapers. She walked into the arms of the doting silver-haired grandfather standing next to the crib.

"How is my precious darling?" she cooed.

"I'm fine," said Tynan. "And—except for a wet diaper—so is your grandson."

Arm in arm, Maude and Tynan beamed down at the blue-eyed baby happily chewing on his toes.

"Who was that on the telephone?" asked Tynan as he expertly replaced the soggy diaper. "Your agent?"

"No. Miranda. She and Stuart finished their errands and are going to dinner at that new restaurant on Sunset Boulevard."

"Too bad," said Tynan. "Guess that means we're stuck with the kid here for a few more hours."

"If we're lucky they may decide to take in a movie after dinner. You know how they feel about the movies." Maude picked up her grandson and cuddled him.

"There's a Bogart-Bacall revival going on at UCLA. I wonder if they know about that."

"Be sure you tell them. It may keep them in town a few more days. I'm not ready for this visit to end." She kissed the baby on its cheek. "I must say, when I sent Miranda after the jewels I never expected . . ."

"What?"

"That my terrible stepson would turn into such a delightful son-in-law."

"Miranda did well, all right. I've got the feeling her first husband will be her last."

"Yes," agreed Maude smugly. "Just like her mother."

\*     \*     \*     \*     \*

# Silhouette
# ROMANCE™

# COMING NEXT MONTH

**#1114 DADDY ON BOARD—Terry Essig**
*Fabulous Fathers*
Lenore Pettit's son needed a father figure, and he picked her boss,
Paul McDaniels. For Tim's sake she agreed to a vacation with
Paul and his daughter. But they could never be a family—could
they?

**#1115 THE COWBOY AND THE PRINCESS—**
**Lindsay Longford**
Hank Tyler had nothing to offer a woman—he'd given up his
heart long ago. And "princess" Gillian Elliott would certainly not
be the exception. But Hank couldn't resist finding out if under the
"princess" image lay a sweet and loving lady....

**#1116 ALONG COMES BABY—Anne Peters**
*First Comes Marriage*
When Ben Kertin found a pregnant woman hiding on his ranch
he couldn't turn her away. Marcie Hillier needed protection, and
marriage seemed the best solution. Until Ben began wishing for
more than a temporary arrangement....

**#1117 WILD WEST WIFE—Jayne Addison**
Josh Spencer would never allow a woman to mess with his
Wild West ranch! He was determined to show Carly Gerard,
his new partner, that rodeos were not for city slickers. Until Josh
began thinking of Carly in very wifely terms.

**#1118 FORTUNE'S BRIDE—Donna Clayton**
Dylan Mitchell had sworn off romance for life; he could take care
of himself and his young daughter without anyone's help. Then
Laura Adams inherited part of his company, and Dylan found
himself falling for this bride of fortune!

**#1119 SECOND CHANCE FAMILY—Laura Anthony**
Single mom Savannah Markum needed help against cattle rustlers,
but she hadn't counted on the inspector being her ex-fiancé,
Matt Forrester. Savannah had vowed never to marry a lawman,
but seeing Matt again made her wonder if their love deserved a
second chance.